BENJAMIN KRITZER

BENJAMIN KRITZER

A NOVEL

Bruce Kimmel

This book is a work of fiction. Places, events, and situations in this story are purely fictional. Any resemblance to actual persons, living or dead, is coincidental.

© 2002 by Bruce Kimmel. All rights reserved.

No part of this book may be reproduced, restored in a retrieval system, or transmitted by means, electronic, mechanical, photocopying, recording, or otherwise, without written consent from the author.

ISBN: 1 4033 0194 8

This book is printed on acid free paper.

Cover painting by Harvey Schmidt.

1st Books - rev. 06/18/02

For Eddie, Mitzi, and Joel,
without whom…
And especially for Jennifer, the one thing I got perfect.

PROLOGUE
Benjamin and the Bad Men

They'd found him. The Bad Men. Somehow, on a blazingly bright spring day in 1958, they'd found ten-year-old Benjamin Kritzer. How? He thought he'd been clever, crafty even, by going to the Picfair movie theater for the Saturday matinee showing of *The Fly* in Cinemascope (not that the Picfair could show real Cinemascope, their screen wasn't big enough, so they simply cut the sides off the end of the picture), but that was beside the point. No, the point was, how had they figured out he'd *be* at the Picfair? Couldn't he just as easily have gone to his two other neighborhood movie theaters, the Lido or the Stadium? Perhaps they'd followed him, although he hadn't taken his usual route, and he'd checked over and over again to make sure he wasn't being followed. Yet he was absolutely certain they were here. Close.

Benjamin was currently upstairs, in the men's room (or the little boy's room as the condescending ushers were so fond of saying). He'd run up there as a result of the scene in *The Fly* in which Mr. Fly's pretty wife removed the mask that was hiding the face of the scientist who had somehow, through science run amok, managed to end up with the head and arm of a fly. And when Benjamin had seen that hideous fly-head with the bulbous bulging eyes and the disgusting mouth and hairy face, well, it was just a little too much for Benjamin Kritzer and he'd run up the aisle as if he were doing the fifty-yard dash (not that he could do the fifty-yard dash—Benjamin Kritzer did not do sports). He'd promptly gone up the long flight of stairs which led to the men's/little boy's room. He was staring out the window to the alleyway below (daydreaming, of course) and that was when he sensed, no *knew*, that they'd found him. The Bad Men. He knew it even though he hadn't actually seen them. But they were there, all right. Waiting for him to come out of the men's/little boy's room. He didn't really know what they wanted, or what they would do to him, but whatever it was it wasn't good. It was bad. After all, they were the Bad Men. And Bad Men did Bad Things.

Benjamin looked out the window to the alley below and wished that he'd had the foresight to bring his Commando Cody Rocket Jacket with him. If he'd had the foresight to do that he could have just turned the knobs on that jacket (On/Off, Up/Down, Slow/Fast) and flown right out the window, thereby putting a tremendous crimp in the Bad Men's plans. But he hadn't had the foresight to bring his Commando Cody Rocket Jacket and even if he had had the foresight to bring his

Commando Cody Rocket Jacket there was the little matter of the bars on the window. Yes, jacket or no jacket, the window was out, escape-wise. Benjamin then looked at the bathroom door. He was quite certain the Bad Men were waiting for him, right at the bottom of the stairs. But what the Bad Men apparently hadn't learned yet was that ten-year-old Benjamin Kritzer was one Crafty Jew. Oh, yes, he was a Crafty Jew, yesireebob, and Crafty Jews were more crafty than Crafty Protestants or Crafty Catholics or any other Crafty People. Benjamin thought long and hard and also hard and long, planning his plan, crafting his craftiness. He could hear the distant sound of children screaming from inside the theater. He could hear the birds outside the window. He could hear his own heart, thud-thudding in his chest. But he knew what he had to do—he'd done it before, it always worked, it was a brilliant diversion. It was, above all, crafty. With great resolve, Benjamin headed towards the door.

He came out of the bathroom like a house afire. Without even looking, he dropped to the ground and rolled down the stairs, clumpety-clumping all the way down, stair after stair, until he reached the bottom where he lay inert, like a piece of his grandfather's whitefish. One of the ushers came up to him.

"Hey, how many times do you have to be told? No rolling down the stairs," said the usher, very very sternly. "Why do you do that? Why do you roll down the stairs like that? It's not normal."

Benjamin looked up at the usher and replied, "The Bad Men were after me. It seemed like a good idea."

"The Bad Men," the usher said, annoyed. "One of these days you're going to hurt yourself, rolling down the stairs like that. We've told you not to do it. Haven't we told you not to do it? One more time and you're not going to be allowed to come here anymore."

The usher helped Benjamin to his feet. Benjamin looked around. No Bad Men. His craftiness had worked once again and once again he was safe and sound. The exasperated usher walked away. Benjamin went to the candy counter, bought some Snow Caps and a box of Chocolate Babies and went back into the auditorium, hoping he'd seen the worst of *The Fly* (he hadn't), knowing he had once again thwarted the Bad Men.

BENJAMIN KRITZER

PART ONE
Childhood Events

"I'm just a kid again,
Doin' what I did again,
Singin' a song
When the red red robin comes
Bob bob bobbin' along"

———*When The Red Red Robin Comes Bob Bob Bobbin' Along*

Bruce Kimmel

CHAPTER ONE
Beginnings

Benjamin Stanley Kritzer was born in 1947 in Los Angeles, California. Even so, he was not around for much of 1947 because before he was even a month old it was already 1948. That was the price one paid for being born in the month of December. Therefore, he could not remember anything whatsoever about the year 1947. Actually, he couldn't remember anything about 1948 either. No, his first real memories were from 1951 and on. Those other years were lost to him. Gone, but presumably filled with diapers, bottles, baby food, drool, various and sundry bathroom functions, first words, first steps—all the usual baby things babies go through. But at some point, around the age of four, Benjamin Kritzer's memory functions kicked in and once they did he could remember *everything*, no matter how tiny the detail. For example, when Benjamin was five, he was rushed to the hospital where he had his tonsils taken out. After receiving the ether, Benjamin had a dream and throughout his entire life he would remember this dream vividly. He dreamed that he was in the hospital having his tonsils taken out, only they were taking them out with an iron, the kind of iron you iron clothes with. His tonsils simply stuck to the iron and were pulled out. He also remembered the vanilla ice cream they gave him when he was well enough to take some food. That's how good his memory was, and he could remember other dreams and actual events just as vividly, years and years after they'd happened.

***

Los Angeles in the early fifties was a strange and wondrous place for a young boy to grow up. Everything about the city reeked of personality. And Benjamin was no different—he reeked of personality, too. Ever since he could remember (and he had an excellent memory), he thought he was unique and special, just like the city he lived in. *Why* he thought that was an enigma to him, but think it he did. He could actually remember being four and thinking, "I'm different than other people. I'm special." It was a funny thing for a four-year-old to think, but he thought it and, more importantly, he believed it. His conviction in his uniqueness and specialness never wavered as he grew up. Also around the age of four he began to be convinced he was an orphan. Why was he convinced of this? Simple: His mother, Minnie Kritzer, was forty-two and his father, Ernest Kritzer, was forty-five when he was born and wasn't that just a little too old to be having children in 1947? Certainly the parents of the other kids in the neighborhood were all much younger than his own. Then there was the fact that there were simply no baby pictures of him anywhere. He asked about this time and again, and his parents always told him they couldn't find the baby pictures. He thought that smelled like a piece of his grandfather's whitefish (bone in—the way his grandfather liked it). There were baby pictures of his psychotic older brother, Jeffrey, plenty of those lying around the house. But all the pictures of Benjamin were from the age of one on. Certainly he wasn't born at the age of one, and certainly most normal parents took pictures of their children prior to being one (Jeffrey being the living proof), so where were Benjamin's baby pictures? Nowhere, that's where, and thus his conviction that he was adopted at the age of one and immediately photographed with the people who were now and who would for always be his parents.

The one thing Benjamin knew from looking at the pictures from when he was one was that he was an incredibly ugly one-year-old. It would be hard to imagine, he thought, an uglier one-year-old child than his very own one-year-old self. But at some point Benjamin had turned into a normal looking child and from then on he was eternally grateful for not having to go through life having a face that dogs would shy away from in the street.

***

The Kritzers resided on Sherbourne Drive, which was located in a nice middle-class Jewish neighborhood. It was a small but nice house. His parents had, at some point, added on a master bedroom in the back, which was very spacious and had huge closets and a huge bed and really ugly furniture. In fact, all the furniture in the house on Sherbourne Drive was ugly. Take, for instance, the swan wallpaper. It was bad enough having swan wallpaper (bad enough that Benjamin didn't want anybody he knew to ever come over), but when that swan wallpaper was bilious green and nauseating pink it was even worse. There was a dining room with a large dining table, a large mirror ornately bordered with silver swans (apparently the swans were a *motif*), and a big ugly china cabinet. At an early age Benjamin learned that one never ate off the plates in the big ugly china cabinet so just what the point of the big ugly china cabinet was eluded him. When he would query his mother about this she would invariably say, "Go play in traffic."

The living room had a brown sofa, a brown upright piano, and a brown television. Benjamin loved that television (it was a twelve-inch screen—huge). He would sometimes wake up very early in the morning so he could watch the test pattern. He was obsessed with the test pattern. He loved the test pattern. To him, the test pattern was the most interesting thing he'd ever seen. He would just stare at it, mesmerized, looking at the Indian and all the little intricate diagrams and numbers. He didn't know what any of it meant, but he was quite certain that that test pattern held the secrets of the universe. When he discussed this with his mother, she would invariably say, "Go play in traffic."

Benjamin shared a bedroom with his insane older brother, Jeffrey Kritzer. Benjamin truly believed that Jeffrey's entire purpose in life was to torment, torture, abuse and otherwise make Benjamin Kritzer's life a living hell. And Jeffrey was very successful at it, oh, yes, he was *very* successful. For example, Jeffrey knew that one of Benjamin's bugaboos was the sound of people chewing their food loudly and obnoxiously. Benjamin hated that, and sitting at the dinner table with his mother, father, and Jeffrey was like the Japanese water torture, whatever that was (he'd seen it in a movie on TV but couldn't remember exactly what the water torture was). The sounds of the Kritzers' eating could be heard for blocks, Benjamin was quite sure of that. So, what Jeffrey would do was this: After the lights were out and they were in bed, Benjamin would be trying to sleep. Then, all of a sudden, he would hear Jeffrey making those hideous eating noises of his, because Jeffrey had brought a banana into the bedroom and was eating that banana as annoyingly as he possibly could. That was the worst sound of all, the eating of a banana. Benjamin hated bananas for that very reason—the sound of it being eaten was grotesque—the gnashing mushing mashing sounds were too much for him. He would lie there, trying to be calm, trying to take it, trying not to let it get to him, but after two minutes of it he would simply start screaming at his brother and threatening to kill him with a knife from the kitchen. This would bring his mother and/or father into the room and they would inquire screamingly why their Benjamin was screaming. Benjamin would scream back that Jeffrey was eating a banana in bed and driving him crazy, but Jeffrey would just sit there all innocent and scream back, "What banana? Do you see a banana?" and of course there would be no banana because Jeffrey had *eaten* the damn thing and now there was no evidence of it ever having been in the room or his mouth. And so Benjamin would get screamed at for screaming at Jeffrey, and Jeffrey would scream just to be annoying, and the whole thing was very unpleasant in the extreme. His parents would always believe Jeffrey over him and that was just further proof that he was adopted.

Another reason Benjamin thought he was adopted was the lack of any resemblance to his parents whatsoever. Ernie Kritzer was five-foot four-inches tall and weighed in around two hundred and fifty pounds, with a round belly and stubby legs. He was bald on top, unless you counted the four strands of hair that he carefully combed over his shiny dome. The hair on the sides was always neatly cut (Ernie had a haircut once a week no matter what, although, given the amount of hair being cut, Benjamin didn't really see the point), he wore glasses with big thick black frames, and he always reeked of Mennen's After Shave. Benjamin, on the other hand, was slight, had hair (and hated to get it cut), didn't reek of Mennen's After Shave and didn't wear glasses with big thick black frames, hence he was about as opposite from Ernie Kritzer as you could get.

Minnie Kritzer was shorter than her husband by four inches and, although not fat, was certainly heavier than she should have been. She had blonde hair (so did Jeffrey), blue eyes (so did Jeffrey) and, like Ernie, she also wore glasses, although her frames were pointy and had rhinestones. She had an ample bosom, fair skin and thin lips. She also had false teeth, both uppers and lowers (Minnie had been plagued by dental problems for years—finally her dentist suggested pulling all her teeth and replacing them with nice brand spanking new ones, all shiny and white). They were very nice teeth indeed, and the fact is that no one would have ever known she had false teeth if it wasn't for her habit of moving them around in her mouth. She'd clack them up and down and sideways and the sight of those ever-moving teeth was always very unnerving to Benjamin. In any case, just as Benjamin looked nothing like Ernie Kritzer, he looked nothing like Minnie Kritzer either (Jeffrey, on the other hand, favored his mother quite a bit). That was a strikeout in the resemblance department, and it only strengthened Benjamin's conviction that he was not the actual child of these actual people.

It seemed to Benjamin that his parents didn't really *like* having children, they just sort of *tolerated* having children, having children was something that was done back then, everyone did it. It wasn't as much fun as playing Canasta or going to Vegas, two of Ernie and Minnie's favorite things to do, but still it was definitely a status thing for them to have their little Kritzer family. Minnie was also an extremely hysterical woman—not hysterical in the sense that she was a laugh riot, but hysterical in the hysterical sense.

Once, when the Kritzers were returning home from dinner, Benjamin and Jeffrey had gone to their room, Ernie had gone to the refrigerator to get some ice water, and Minnie had gone to her bedroom to get undressed. A moment later a blood-curdling scream issued forth from the bedroom, the kind of blood-curdling scream that would lead you to believe Minnie Kritzer was either having a knife thrust into her eyeball or that her teeth had gone missing. She came running from the bedroom at full tilt, dressed only in her girdle and brassiere, screaming like a banshee. Benjamin and Jeffrey ran out of their room to see what was happening and Ernie came running from the kitchen. She paused her scream just long enough to tell everyone what the matter was—and what the matter was was simply this: A mouse. Minnie Kritzer had seen a mouse and this little scurrying rodent had caused Minnie Kritzer to become a screaming lunatic. She continued to scream for a full five minutes until Ernie Kritzer had thrown a dress over her head and bundled the entire Kritzer clan to a nearby motel on La Cienega. The next day the exterminators came and presumably put an end to the short sweet life of Minnie's mouse. When Benjamin later brought the incident up, Minnie refused to acknowledge it, and instead suggested that Benjamin go play in traffic.

There were certain things about the Sherbourne Drive house that gave Benjamin the willies. For example, there was the very large Hoover vacuum cleaner, a very scary-looking machine that made hideous sucking whooshing noises, which, to Benjamin, made the machine sound like it was speaking. Speaking to him personally. "Come here little person and I'll vacuum you up," it would wheeze at him and he would run and hide in his closet. Another thing that gave him the willies was the shower in the bathroom that he and his brother used. That shower was the stuff of nightmares. It was never, as far as Benjamin knew, ever used as a shower. He and his brother only took baths in that bathroom. The shower that people showered in was in his parents' bedroom. No, this shower was used for storage and what was stored in there was horrifying to Benjamin—various plungers and hot water bottles and rubber hoses and weird implements that made Benjamin nauseous whenever he thought about them. He'd queried his mother about those plungers and hot water bottles and hoses and weird implements once, and his mother used a word that Benjamin never wanted to hear again: Enema. He just didn't like the sound of that word at all.

Around this time, Benjamin also decided that he wouldn't take any more baths, he would only take showers in his parents' bedroom. When his mother asked him why, he told her that he didn't like the thought of lying in his own dirt. She thought about that for a minute, threatened to use the hanger on him, but saw there was no dissuading Benjamin from the no bath business. She immediately fell onto the couch weeping, crying out forlornly, "What did I do to deserve this?"

***

In 1955, Benjamin attended a triple bill at his beloved Lido Theater. The three features were *Creature With the Atom Brain*, *Devil Girl From Mars* and *Invaders From Mars*. The first two were not very good, Benjamin thought, but he absolutely loved *Invaders From Mars*. After viewing it, Benjamin became convinced that his parents, like the parents in the film, had become Martianized, had had little "x" things put in their necks, which is what those evil Martians did to Earth people to Martianize them. And once those little "x" things had been put into their necks, people didn't behave the same. That was the only logical way to explain his parents' sometimes bizarre behavior. How else to explain the way his father's tongue would suddenly protrude from his mouth when he got ready to spank the brothers Kritzer? Yes, that tongue would fly out of his father's mouth, waving like an out-of-control salami, and that lolling tongue meant it was time for the brothers Kritzer to amscray but quick. How else to explain a father who would come home from work, insist that the Kritzer family eat at five o'clock, then sit in his chair the rest of the night watching television in only his pajama top and nothing else. That was simply grotesque to Benjamin Kritzer, seeing his father sitting in that chair, pajama top barely covering his rotund stomach, with his dinkle lying there like a dead herring for all to see. How else to explain parents who even *used* the word "dinkle", or, even worse, "wee wee", when referring to a boy part? How else to explain a father who would take his family to the movies and, as soon as the show began, would immediately fall asleep, snoring so loudly they could probably hear him in Pomona? In fact, Benjamin and Jeffrey would always move way down in front so that no one would think they were with the Snorer from the Black Lagoon. How else to explain his mother's penchant for using a wooden hanger to punish him for his many and varied misdeeds? How else to explain a mother who would try to get her children to drink milk en vasser, milk served in hot water with sugar. Just thinking about that drink made Benjamin want to vomit on the ground. Yes, what kind of parents did these things unless they'd been Martianized and had had little "x" things put in their necks? And while Benjamin never did find visual evidence of those little "x" things, he was most positive they were there.

***

During summer, when he wasn't in school, a typical Benjamin Kritzer day would begin at Leo's Delicatessen, which was a few blocks from his house. He loved Leo's Delicatessen and he thought Leo himself was the nicest man alive. Much nicer than his brother Jeffrey and, if truth be told, much nicer than his parents. Every morning, Benjamin would walk to Leo's and purchase his morning soda pop—most likely a Coca Cola, but sometimes a Dad's Root Beer or, if he were feeling bold, a Nehi Orange Soda. He loved bottles of soda pop and he collected the bottle caps. Quite an impressive collection if he did say so himself and he did at every opportunity. Leo always had some extra bottle caps for him and even an occasional free pickle from the pickle barrel.

After Leo's, Benjamin would usually head over to Ralph's Five and Dime and maybe buy some caps for his Fanner 50 or maybe just look around and see what was new. Sometimes he'd go next door to Big Town market and have one of their delicious slices of pizza. Then it was south on La Cienega, over to the miniature golf course where he might or might not play a game (he was very good), past Fosters Freeze and Marty's Bike and Candy Shop (where they had the best red licorice in the world—or at least on La Cienega) and over to the Adohr Farms bottling plant on the corner of 18th and La Cienega, just a few blocks from his house.

During his seventh year, Benjamin had made an incredible discovery while nosing around the Adohr Farms bottling plant. He found a back area where they kept their broken and discarded delivery trucks.

Benjamin loved sneaking back there and playing on the trucks, pretending to drive them, shifting the big gearshift doohickey. Then, one day he was playing on one of the trucks and he pushed a button and, miracle of miracles, the ignition actually turned over and the engine was running. Benjamin pushed the big doohickey and managed to put the thing into gear and the truck lurched forward, smashing into the truck in front of it. Gears grinding loudly, he shoved the doohickey backwards as hard as he could and suddenly the truck went into reverse, lurching backwards and smashing into the truck in back of it. He spent the next hour going back and forth, smashing into the two trucks like some delivery truck driver gone horribly amok. Back and forth, smash, smash, over and over, laughing himself silly until he finally had to stop because if he'd laughed any harder he was going to die right there in that lurching Adohr delivery truck.

***

Benjamin didn't have a lot of friends. Not real friends anyway. Oh, he'd sometimes play with the neighborhood kids, but he didn't really like them and he thought they were idiots; however, they were occasionally okay to be around, especially if you could use their pool. One of them, Paul Needle, who lived two houses away, was fond of taking a raw egg, poking a hole in it, and then sucking out the contents within. What could you do with a person like that, someone who would poke a hole in an egg and suck out that gelatinous guck from within and gulp it down as if it were a chocolate malt? That just made Benjamin Kritzer want to vomit on the ground. No, Benjamin didn't have a lot of time for those kinds of friends. Besides, the kids in his neighborhood were all little troublemakers and would occasionally tell Benjamin's mother that Benjamin had done or said something he really hadn't done or said. And, of course, Minnie Kritzer, being a Martian, would believe them and out would come the wooden hanger and she'd hit Benjamin with it several times and then she'd fall on the sofa weeping. Since Benjamin had been the one who'd gotten hit with the wooden hanger, this weeping mother routine seemed very strange to him. So, Benjamin was pretty much a loner. He would stay inside and watch TV (*My Little Margie*, *Racket Squad* and *Highway Patrol* were some of his favorites), or he would go off to the movies and get lost in the myriad adventures he saw depicted on the giant screen. He wanted to *be* in those adventures, wanted to be up there on that giant screen. He would daydream and play those adventures when he got home. He'd be John Wayne piloting an airplane and whistling *The High and the Mighty* (they had a 78rpm record of the music—Benjamin was fascinated by the name of the "whistler" listed on the label, Muzzy Marcellino), he'd be Ray Milland in *Lisbon*, he'd be Joel McCrea in *Wichita*. He especially loved movies in Cinemascope and VistaVision. He loved seeing those logos on the screen and, when he'd get home, he'd spend hours drawing movie screens with curtains and the Cinemascope and VistaVision logos.

BENJAMIN KRITZER

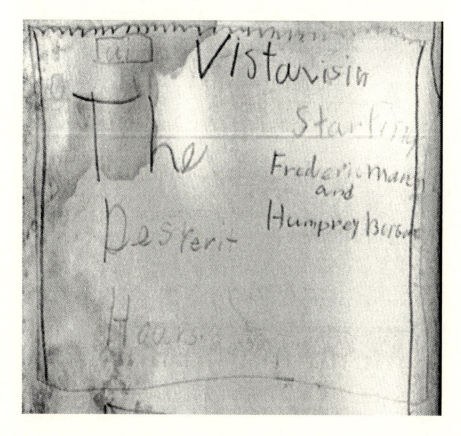

Yes, Benjamin loved movies and he loved movie theaters. He loved roaming the lobbies and the lounges and loved sitting in the dark in row ten (always row ten, first seat on the aisle), listening to the music they played before the double feature began, waiting for the beautiful drapes to open and reveal the screen. His favorite movie theaters were the Village in Westwood—whose Cinemascope screen was so huge his eyes could barely take it all in—and the Wiltern on Western and Wilshire, with its stunning décor, two balconies, downstairs lounge (with a huge staircase, perfect for rolling down), and its two sets of curtains, ones that went up and ones that parted to reveal the magnificent screen. But he even loved the Picfair with its tiny screen and no curtains. They were all exotic palaces to him, where he could escape into new and exciting worlds. Benjamin was *so* movie crazy that when his father would get tickets to see the Hollywood Stars baseball team at Gilmore Field (next to Benjamin's beloved Farmer's Market) he would make his father get seats that faced east, toward the movie screen of the Gilmore Drive-In. That way Benjamin wouldn't have to be bored to tears by baseball and could watch whatever was being shown on the screen of the drive-in. Of course, there was no sound, but that was even better, because Benjamin could then make up his own movie to go along with the images he was seeing. He'd do different voices for the different characters, provide sound effects, all out loud much to the embarrassment of his brother and parents, not to mention the annoyance of those sitting around him trying to concentrate on the baseball game.

***

Around that time Benjamin also started doing his famous death scenes. Whenever his parents would take him somewhere, Benjamin would die in some elaborate way—there was no reason for this, he just enjoyed dying elaborately. One party his parents took him to (and regretted having brought him immediately) was especially memorable. The minute they walked in the door, Benjamin had started weaving as if he'd been shot with a twelve-gauge shotgun, bobbing this way and that way, lurching like the Adohr truck, bounding against the walls while the guests looked at him as if he were one of those communists that Richard Carlson was always ferreting out on *I Led Three Lives*—until he finally did an amazing rollover on the couch and hit the floor with a resounding thud. He lay there dead for the next two hours. People had to step over him and they would say things like, "Aren't you tired of this silly game?" but of course Benjamin was dead and could hardly answer them. After a time, his parents simply stopped taking him to parties.

Bruce Kimmel

***

Every day at noon he would watch Sheriff John on TV. Sheriff John was a local children's television show host and his show went out live every single weekday at noon, hence the name *Sheriff John's Lunch Brigade*. Benjamin loved Sheriff John who, like Leo from the delicatessen, was just really and truly a nice person. Sheriff John would look out from the TV screen and it was almost as if he were talking to Benjamin Kritzer personally. In fact, Benjamin pretty much believed the Sheriff *was* talking to him personally. Just like Benjamin wanted to be in those movie adventures, he also wanted to be like Sheriff John, he wanted to host his own *Lunch Brigade* show. To that end, Benjamin set up a folding table by the TV, and he made a TV camera (he'd seen a picture of one in a magazine) out of the cardboard in his father's laundered shirts, placed it on the folding table and pretended he was Sheriff Benjamin—he'd do the whole show just like Sheriff John did. Complete with commercials for Kellogg's Sugar Pops ("Sugar Pops are tops").

Occasionally, Benjamin would take his camera outside, on location, and hold it in front of him and do a live broadcast from his neighborhood. The neighbors would not know quite what to make of this, but were usually good-natured enough to take part in the broadcast. Except for Mrs. Bruno, who would say pithy things like, "Why are you pointing that big bunch of taped-up cardboard at yourself, you weird little boy?" Benjamin would, of course, just ignore Mrs. Bruno, because that's what one did—otherwise Mrs. Bruno, who had a rather severe moustache and wore rubber gloves, might put you into the trunk of her 1941 De Soto, at least so the legend went.

***

One day, Benjamin was in the car with his father and as they drove past the Uptown Market Benjamin could not believe his eyes. For there, parked in front of the market, was the Oscar Mayer Wienermobile, with a crowd of people gathered around. Benjamin begged his father to stop so that Benjamin could see the Wienermobile up close (he'd seen the Wienermobile on television many times, but this was *in person*). Ernie found a parking space and he and Benjamin got out of the car and walked over to join the crowd. The Wienermobile was amazing with its huge wiener sitting atop its mobile, and Benjamin marveled at it. And as if that wasn't enough, there, live and also in person, was Little Oscar himself. Benjamin, who'd seen Little Oscar on Sheriff John, was beside himself with excitement. Little Oscar (who looked like one of the Munchkins) was throwing Wiener whistles to the crowd of kids and Ernie managed to catch one for Benjamin. Benjamin also noticed that there was a big bowl of jelly beans on a table because there was a contest going on—whichever child guessed closest to the correct number of jelly beans would make a guest appearance on the *Rocky Jones–Space Ranger* television show. So, Ernie filled out the form and Benjamin gave him a number to fill in—356 jelly beans was Benjamin's guess (why that was his guess he had no idea—it just seemed like a good number to guess)—and Ernie deposited the form in the entry box. Little Oscar gave out autographs (Benjamin got one) and told all the kids and parents to buy all the delicious Oscar Mayer products. Then Little Oscar got into the Wienermobile and he and the giant wiener car drove off down the street.

***

Two days later the Kritzers received a phone call telling them that Benjamin Kritzer had won the jelly-bean-counting contest and that he would be making an appearance on the *Rocky Jones–Space Ranger* show. Ernie was instructed to deliver Benjamin to the television studio promptly at six o'clock in the evening the following Thursday.

That week the days positively *crawled* by, they occurred in slow motion, each day longer than the last. Finally Thursday arrived and the Kritzers crowded into their ritzy new Oldsmobile (the Ford simply would *not* do) and headed to Hollywood. Once at the studio and parked, Ernie, Minnie (who'd had her hair done and everything), Jeffrey and Benjamin were ushered into the studio. There were people everywhere, moving lights and equipment, and it was all very exciting to see. As they were led to the set, Benjamin marveled at the television cameras, real television cameras and, as good as his cardboard replica of a television camera was, it was nothing like this. As they reached the set, the person who'd ushered them there told Ernie, Minnie and Jeffrey to gather around a television monitor so they could watch Benjamin's appearance. Then, a very gruff man who called himself a stage manager took Benjamin onto the set where he was introduced to the actors. He couldn't believe it—there was Rocky Jones himself, with his space gun, shaking Benjamin's very own hand. Benjamin was shown where to stand and was told not to move from that position. The three television cameras moved in closer and someone was saying something like, "We're live in five, four, three, two…"

"Who do we have here today, Rocky?" said one of the Space Rangers. Rocky looked over at Benjamin and said, "This is Benjamin Kritzer and he's come to visit us in our rocket ship. How are you today, Benjamin?" Benjamin, never at a loss for words, was suddenly at a loss for words. He stood there, staring dumbly at Rocky Jones. "Benjamin? Did you have a nice trip up here to outer space?" Benjamin gulped loudly, finally found his voice, and then answered.

"Yes, we took the Oldsmobile."

One of the Space Rangers started to laugh, which started another Space Ranger laughing and soon Rocky Jones–Space Ranger was laughing although Benjamin didn't quite see what was so funny. Finally, Rocky Jones told Benjamin that, because he was the contest winner, he was going to get a year's supply of Oscar Mayer products and a brand spanking new pair of Buster Brown shoes. As Rocky Jones was saying this, one of the other Space Rangers was handing Benjamin packages of Oscar Mayer Bologna, Liverwurst and Pickle and Pimento Loaf (Benjamin did not like the look of the Pickle and Pimento Loaf one bit) and a Buster Brown shoebox (with a picture of his little dog Tige on the box—just like in the ads). Rocky Jones–Space Ranger thanked Benjamin for visiting and then looked directly at the camera and said, "We'll be back after a word from Oscar Mayer."

The gruff stage manager man came and escorted Benjamin and his armful of prizes off the set. And then the gruff stage manager man gruffly took those prizes right out of Benjamin Kritzer's arms and told the Kritzers that those were only props and that the real prizes would be sent directly to their house in a few weeks. Well, Benjamin wasn't having any of *that* story and he promptly kicked the gruff stage manager man in the shins. Minnie promptly apologized on Benjamin's behalf and told the gruff stage manager man that Benjamin didn't understand the concept of props. Benjamin wondered what there was to understand; to him it was very simple—they'd given him something and then taken it away. If that's what props were all about then he wanted nothing whatsoever to do with props ever again.

Three weeks later, the Kritzers received a year's supply of Oscar Mayer products—boxes and boxes of Oscar Mayer products—so many Oscar Mayer products that the Kritzers gave most of those products to their friends, especially the Pickle and Pimento Loaf. The Buster Brown shoes (with a picture of his little dog Tige on the box) never arrived.

***

And so, the unique Benjamin Kritzer's days and nights passed by—he went to school, he played, he ate, he endured his Martian parents and his brother Jeffrey. He endured the hanger and the daily annoyances and irksome things that might happen because, basically, when all was said and done, Benjamin liked his world. Especially the Helms Truck.

Every day he would listen for the whistle of the Helms Bakery Truck and as soon as he heard it he'd run outside and yell, "Hey, Helms man!" so that that wonderful yellow and blue truck would stop. As he'd approach the truck he could smell the donuts and the freshly baked breads and rolls—it was a smell you couldn't forget, and it permeated the air with a sweetness that was beyond belief. He'd board the truck and ask to look at the donuts, and the Helms man, in his perfectly tailored and laundered Helms uniform, would open the drawers containing the donuts. Benjamin would look at that magnificent assortment of glazed donuts, jelly donuts, powdered sugar donuts, crumb donuts; he'd stare at each and every one longingly and lovingly and then he would invariably purchase the chocolate donut because that was his favorite, that chocolate donut was just the best thing in the whole wide world. Oh, he'd tried the jelly donut, and the glazed donuts were awfully tasty, but nothing came close to that chocolate donut, that chocolate donut was heaven on earth as far as Benjamin Kritzer was concerned. And then there was the Good Humor Ice Cream Truck, with its familiar tune echoing in the air as it would drive down Sherbourne Drive, and he and the other neighborhood kids would run outside and buy whatever ice cream bars suited their fancy that particular day (Benjamin had been on a Creamsicle kick for almost a year).

Yes, Benjamin's World was filled with daily wonders and adventures—he was eight years old and, as Minnie Kritzer would put it, happy as a clam. But soon all his adventures heretofore would pale in comparison with what the next two years would hold.

CHAPTER TWO

The Arrival of the Bad Men, and Grandpa Kritzer and the Commando Cody Rocket Jacket

The spring of 1956 was the spring when the Bad Men first appeared. How it happened was this: One day Benjamin had come home after school and he'd found his mother lying on her bed, her eyes covered with pads soaked in Witch Hazel (never a good sign), crying hysterically

"… *what did I do to deserve this?*"

and next to her was his father, strangely home at 3:30 in the afternoon. Benjamin, being naturally inquisitive at the sight of his mother lying on the bed crying hysterically with Witch Hazel-soaked pads on her eyes, and his father strangely home at 3:30 in the afternoon, asked what the matter was. "Benjamin, please, go play in traffic," his mother said, tears streaming down her cheeks from beneath the Witch Hazel pads. It was then that Benjamin noticed that all the dresser drawers in the bedroom had been pulled out, with the contents scattered on the floor and the entire room looking like it had been hit by a tornado.

"We've been robbed," his mother wailed. "They took my jewelry, they took my mad money, they took *everything*."

Benjamin asked who "they" were. "The Bad Men," replied his father. "The Bad Men who robbed our house." Before Benjamin could process that information, there was a knock at the door. His father went and answered it, with Benjamin dogging his footsteps. It was a policeman. A real policeman in a real uniform, with a real gun in a real holster. The real policeman went into the master bedroom where he took a report on the robbery from Ernie and the sobbing Minnie. The real policeman told everyone not to touch anything until the Fingerprint Man got there. Benjamin liked the sound of that—Fingerprint Man— and wondered if, when he grew up, he might even *be* a Fingerprint Man. There was something about the sound of "Fingerprint Man" that sounded important. Benjamin Kritzer, Fingerprint Man.

After the real policeman left and the real Fingerprint Man had left (any appeal that being a Fingerprint Man might have had evaporated the minute Benjamin saw the squat, sweaty, ugly little Fingerprint Man), and Minnie had calmed down (she'd taken one of her "special" pills), and Jeffrey had tired of trying to scare Benjamin with dark tales of the Bad Men, the Kritzers, exhausted from their ordeal, retired for the evening.

Sometime in the middle of the night, Benjamin awoke, sweating, heart beating loudly in his small chest. In the far-off distance, he could hear sirens roaring distantly somewhere in the city. But he always heard that when he'd awaken in the middle of the night. There were always sirens roaring distantly somewhere in the city, just like on *Dragnet* or *Highway Patrol*. But that wasn't all he was hearing. He was hearing footsteps in the dining room. Creaking footsteps. One, then another. Then he heard the china cabinet rattling as if someone (the Bad Men?) were opening it. Benjamin's heart was pounding now—he wanted to wake Jeffrey up to tell him, but he was afraid if he spoke that the Bad Men would hear him and come down the hall and do something horrible to him and Jeffrey. Well, it would be okay if they did something horrible to Jeffrey, he deserved something horrible for all the banana eating torture, but it would not be okay if they did something horrible to Benjamin because Benjamin was unique, special. So, he lay there, mute, sweating, his heart beating out more rhythm than Bill Haley's *Rock Around The Clock*. What were they doing, the Bad Men? Hadn't they taken enough that afternoon? Had they gotten home with all their stolen treasure and thought, "Wait, we left the china?" and had they then come back to the very same house they'd already robbed? That was rather bold of the Bad Men but then Bad Men were bold, Benjamin supposed, and there was nothing you could do about it except lie there and pray they'd leave soon. He could still hear the creaking footsteps (were they getting closer? Were they coming down the hallway?), creaking, creaking…

The next thing Benjamin knew, he was being ruthlessly shaken out of a sound sleep. He didn't remember falling asleep after hearing the Bad Men trying to steal the china, but he must have because he was being ruthlessly shaken out of a sound sleep. His eyes bugged open, focused, and saw his mother looking haggard and weary.

"Did they take all the china?" Benjamin asked.

His mother looked at him wearily. "What are you talking about? Did who take all the china?"

Benjamin sat up and rubbed his eyes. "I heard them," he said. "The Bad Men—they came back last night and I heard them taking the china."

"You were having a bad dream. No one came back to take the china. They're probably *in* China by now with all my jewelry and mad money and everything." And with that she burst into tears, crying forlornly, "What did I do to deserve this?"

"I wasn't having a bad dream, I heard them, they were here. The Bad Men. They were stealing the china."

Minnie pulled Benjamin out of the bed and took him into the dining room. "There. What do you see? I see china. Do you see china?"

And sure enough, all the china was in place, nothing was missing. But it hadn't been a dream, Benjamin was absolutely sure about that. Benjamin had heard the footsteps, had heard the china cabinet open. His mother had that hanger look in her eye so Benjamin beat a hasty retreat back to the bedroom, dressed hurriedly, and went off to school. The entire way there he was quite certain he was being followed by the Bad Men.

Bruce Kimmel

***

From then on, Benjamin would frequently awaken in the middle of the night, hear the distant sirens wailing somewhere deep in the city, and without fail would hear the creaking footsteps in the dining room, hear the china cabinet being opened, hear the Bad Men in his house most assuredly robbing the Kritzers blind once again. He would lie there, paralyzed with fear, afraid to move even an inch, afraid to call out to his sleeping brother (why didn't Jeffrey hear what was going on?). He would eventually fall asleep, only to wake up in the morning and find the china cabinet and its contents undisturbed. Ultimately he decided the Bad Men were having sport with him, were tormenting him, would eventually *get* him. This feeling rarely left him and he spent much of his time looking over his shoulder (never seeing them, of course—they were much too clever for that) and watching his back.

***

Benjamin's favorite relative was Grandpa Kritzer. Samuel Kritzer was a sweet old man, bald like his son Ernie, but unlike Ernie, thin and tall. He always wore a short-sleeve shirt and always had his favorite fedora on his head. Grandpa Kritzer clearly doted on Benjamin. Benjamin's mother would drop him off at Grandpa Kritzer's apartment just off Fairfax, and the two of them would walk over to The Bagel and eat lunch and then would go on to the Saturday matinee at the Picfair. It was with Grandpa Kritzer that Benjamin had first discovered Commando Cody, in an exciting serial ("12 Thrilling Chapters!") called *Radar Men From the Moon*. Benjamin loved coming back to the theater every Saturday with Grandpa Kritzer to see the next chapter. Most of all, Benjamin loved Commando Cody's Rocket Jacket, an amazing leather affair with two rockets on the back and a control panel on the front with three knobs. By turning the knobs (On/Off, Up/Down, Slow/Fast), Commando Cody could fly through the sky, soaring over the city, zooming around among the clouds. Benjamin wanted that Rocket Jacket more than anything because he wanted to fly more than anything. He wanted to fly through the sky and soar over the city and zoom around among the clouds.

His obsession with being able to fly began with Superman on television and, when he was seven, he even had his own Superman outfit. Once, while wearing it, he decided he was going to fly and he climbed a ladder to the top of the garage. His mother saw him climbing up to the garage roof and came running out of the house and into the yard, screaming at him to get down from there. Benjamin looked at his screaming mother, but it was too late, he'd made up his mind and much to her horror he proceeded to leap from the garage roof, arms outstretched. With cape billowing, he promptly and speedily crashed to the backyard lawn. Fortunately, it was a short drop and Benjamin sustained not even a bruise, unless you count the black-and-blue mark where his mother hit him with the hanger for doing such a dangerous thing. The lessons he learned from his abortive leap were a) that he wasn't Superman, and b) that he was truly beginning to dislike his mother for hitting him with the hanger. In fact, he refused to cry when she did it, no matter how much it hurt, because it made her angry and frustrated (what good was it if you hit someone with a hanger and they didn't cry?), and if he was going to endure the hanger then making her angry and frustrated because he didn't cry was his small reward. It reminded him of that movie he'd seen, *I'll Cry Tomorrow* with Susan Hayward, where the little girl in the first scene was smacked around by her mother and then learned not to cry (or at least not to cry until tomorrow). The song from that movie, *When the Red, Red Robin Comes Bob, Bob, Bobbin' Along* became Benjamin's favorite and he sang it over and over again.

So, having learned the lesson that he wasn't Superman, Benjamin then became determined to have a Rocket Jacket like Commando Cody. First of all, having a Rocket Jacket like Commando Cody meant that Benjamin could easily escape from the Bad Men and that was reason enough to need one. Grandpa Kritzer knew about the Bad Men and Benjamin's desire to have a Commando Cody Rocket Jacket. One day, Grandpa Kritzer came over and brought a gift for Benjamin—a real imitation leather coat, which looked just like Commando Cody's. Benjamin couldn't believe it and he gave Grandpa Kritzer the biggest hug and kiss he could muster. He and Grandpa Kritzer then set about making two rockets for the back (using two cylindrical-shaped buttermilk containers painted silver) and the control panel for the front (like his TV camera, made of cardboard from his father's laundered shirts) complete with On/Off, Up/Down, and Slow/Fast knobs. Benjamin practically lived in that jacket and would zoom around the house, arms outstretched, making flying noises (he made the *best* flying noises—

(*"tshewwwwwwwwwwwwwwwwwwwwwwwwwwwwwwwwwwwwwww"*) perfect flying noises, which sounded just like Superman flying. After he'd traversed the house, he'd go outside and fly through the neighborhood (*"tshewwwwwwwwwwwwwwwwwwwwwwwwwwwwwwwwwwww"*) until he could fly no more, at which point he'd make himself a nice big glass of milk with Bosco. Benjamin hated milk, but Bosco, that gooey chocolate syrup, at least made it tolerable.

***

In May of 1956, Grandpa Kritzer passed away, and even though Benjamin didn't really understand "passed away", Minnie made it quite clear that Grandpa Kritzer had gone to heaven and that Benjamin wouldn't be seeing him ever again.

That was doubly sad for Benjamin, because he loved Grandpa Kritzer, and because that meant that he was left with two grandparents who, for want of a better word, were the most peculiar grandparents ever put on earth.

CHAPTER THREE
Ocean Park

Gus and Dottie Gelfinbaum, Benjamin's grandparents on his mother's side, lived at the Hotel St. Regis, which was located on the boardwalk at Ocean Park, which was located in Santa Monica. Dottie Gelfinbaum, who was sixty-nine years old and looked eighty-nine, weighed in the neighborhood of three hundred pounds and always dressed in black. She also sat in a big black chair and it was impossible to tell where she left off and the chair began. Gus Gelfinbaum was a crotchety old man of seventy (he also looked eighty-nine) who smoked big smelly cigars relentlessly, spit on the ground relentlessly, and whose favorite things to do were to watch *Amos 'n Andy* and to play Pinochle at the Pinochle Parlor which was located across the street from the Hotel St. Regis. Gus and Dottie had moved from Brooklyn to Chicago, and then on to Los Angeles in the late twenties with their two daughters, Minnie and Lena. When Lena got married and Minnie had moved out, the Gelfinbaums moved to the Hotel St. Regis, where they'd lived ever since.

During the summers, the Kritzers would visit Grandma and Grandpa Gelfinbaum every Tuesday and Thursday. They'd arrive at noon, get on the very scary Hotel St. Regis elevator and go up to the third floor apartment.

The apartment had a living room and a second room which had a Murphy bed and which doubled as a dining room. There was a small kitchen whose windows overlooked the boardwalk and there was a small bathroom. The apartment always smelled of salmon, raw onions and vinegar, the Gelfinbaums' favorite meal. It also seemed totally oppressive, dark and musty. Both Gus and Dottie had thick Yiddish accents and actually spoke to each other in Yiddish a lot of the time. Even though Benjamin couldn't understand what they were saying, it was eminently clear that for all intents and purposes they could not stand each other, in Yiddish, English or any other language.

Grandma Gelfinbaum was very fond of pinching the brothers Kritzers' cheeks, and she did not do this lightly—no, she grabbed those cheeks and pinched them as if she were molding clay, usually while kvelling "sheyne punim" (pretty face) as loudly as she could. She would then give them each gelt in the form of a quarter or, if she was feeling generous, a half dollar.

During meals, no matter what type of food was put in front of Grandpa Gelfinbaum, be it brisket, chicken, or even dessert, he would always say, "What is it, fish?" He did this without fail and Benjamin and Jeffrey would begin to laugh uncontrollably as each dish was brought to the table. A corned beef sandwich? "What is it, fish?" Sweet and sour cabbage? "What is it, fish?" Chicken in a pot? "What is it, fish?" Noodle kugel? "What is it, fish?" No one ever questioned Grandpa Gelfinbaum as to *why* he always said, "What is it, fish?" but say it he did, over and over and over, like a broken what-is-it-fish record.

The other thing Grandpa Gelfinbaum liked to do was to have everyone in the family come into the bathroom to look at his stools. Apparently, making a stool was an ordeal for Grandpa Gelfinbaum (one could occasionally hear him in the bathroom making the most awful noises) and when he finally made a stool it was such a victory that he wanted everyone to see his handiwork. Into the bathroom everyone would parade to view the specimen while Grandpa Gelfinbaum stood to the side, beaming proudly. During one memorable Jewish holiday, the entire family was gathered around the table, eating. Grandpa Gelfinbaum had excused himself right after finishing the gefilte fish and gone into the bathroom to sit on the toilet "like so much fish." Fifteen minutes later, just as the garlic chicken was being served, Grandpa Gelfinbaum emerged from the bathroom and announced, "There's blood in my stool. Everyone, come look, there's blood in my stool." Arguing was hopeless, and so the entire family dutifully arose and entered the bathroom single file to pay homage to Grandpa Gelfinbaum's bloody stool. By the time everyone had made the pilgrimage and had returned to the table, Grandpa Gelfinbaum had already finished most of the what-is-it-fish garlic chicken.

***

The best thing about visiting Grandma and Grandpa Gelfinbaum was going to the Ocean Park Pier. Benjamin loved Ocean Park Pier with its brightly lit seediness, and its rides and cotton candy and vanilla custard ice cream and games. Ocean Park Pier at night was absolutely magical. There were sailors in their starched whites, pretty girls in their flowery dresses blowing in the ocean breeze, kids screaming on the rickety rollercoaster; everywhere you looked the pier was pulsing with an amazing potpourri of people and rides and food. And the best thing about Grandpa Gelfinbaum (if there was a best thing) was that he was part of the pier—he owned a giant roulette wheel stand (the Wheel O' Fortune) and people would step right up and spin the giant wheel, place their dime on a number and root loudly as the Wheel O' Fortune went round and round. Most of the time they lost, but sometimes if a really comely young lady was playing, then that comely young lady would most likely go home a winner with a cute little teddy bear tucked under her comely arm (not like the arm on Grandma Gelfinbaum—"just like the jelly on grandma's shelf," Grandpa Gelfinbaum used to cackle, as Dottie's fleshy arms would jiggle).

The Wheel O' Fortune was located directly next to the Vanilla Custard Ice Cream stand and oh how Benjamin loved those Vanilla Custard Ice Cream cones. The flavor and the texture were indescribably wonderful and Benjamin could eat two of them in one visit if left to his own devices, which he frequently was.

Benjamin's favorite things on the pier were the penny arcade, where he could play Skeeball and other games for hours, a ride called Toonerville, the horse racing game, the merry-go-round with its brightly painted horses (Benjamin so wanted to grab the brass ring but he was simply too small and would almost fall off the horse trying to reach for it), and the House of Mirrors with the huge fat lady sitting atop it, endlessly and maniacally laughing at some secret joke that only she was in on. Benjamin also loved pitching pennies to try to win a two-dollar bill and damned if he hadn't actually won one once and he displayed that two-dollar bill proudly in his room for years.

But his *favorite* favorite thing at Ocean Park was the Dome Theater, a gorgeous movie palace located on the boardwalk where one entered the main part of the pier walkway. It was grandiose, with a majestic dome sitting atop the roof. He went to the movies there as often as he could, and they even had stereophonic sound when they showed Cinemascope pictures. Benjamin had especially loved *Beneath the Twelve Mile Reef* on that huge screen—it was almost as if you were down there in the ocean with Robert Wagner and Terry Moore. At the other end of the boardwalk, closer to the really seedy Venice Pier, was another movie theater, the Rosemary. But the Rosemary was boarded up and had been closed since the late forties. Still, like all movie theaters, the Rosemary held a magical allure for Benjamin, and he dreamed of sneaking into the boarded up theater so he could watch movies any time he liked. Once, while walking past it with Grandpa Gelfinbaum, he asked if his grandfather would buy it for him. In answer, Grandpa Gelfinbaum took the slimy wet cigar out of his mouth, hocked a glob of spit on the pavement and said, "What is it, fish?"

In the fall of 1956, Grandpa Gelfinbaum received some startling news—the Ocean Park pier was going to be closed down, to be replaced by a brand new amusement park to be called Pacific Ocean Park—sort of a Disneyland at the beach. This meant the end of the Wheel O' Fortune and most of the other rides and attractions, which would all be razed, come spring of 1957. There would be no place for Grandpa Gelfinbaum or his Wheel O' Fortune or his beloved Pinochle Parlor. No, he would retire and spend the rest of his days sitting on the couch like so much fish, watching soap operas and eating fatty meats and looking at Dottie Gelfinbaum as if she were a large fetid wart.

CHAPTER FOUR
The Erro,
and Nude Living

The Kritzers loved to eat. For Benjamin and Jeffrey that was fine, because they had good child metabolisms and no matter how much they ate they remained thin. Ernie and Minnie, however, had no metabolism, did no exercise and therefore were not thin (although Minnie did enjoy watching every housewife's favorite exercise instructor, Jack LaLanne, on television—Benjamin thought he looked like an upside down bowling pin in a jump suit). Even though Minnie was a good cook (brisket being her specialty), the Kritzers loved eating out, and so, with kids in tow, off they'd go to their neighborhood favorites: Casa Cienega for Mexican, Pete 'n Percy's for barbeque (Benjamin loved

Pete 'n Percy's because they had sawdust on the floor), Gaby's or Stat's for coffee shop food, Kelbo's for ribs, Wan-Q or Kowloon for Chinese, and Hody's because Benjamin liked the clown menu that kids got to order from.

There was always plenty of food in the Kritzer house (certainly there was a preponderance of Oscar Mayer product in the freezer), and that included the ubiquitous hanging salami on the porch. How the Kritzers loved salami, the harder the better. The salami would hang from a nail on a wall near the washer and dryer. Ernie often cut himself off large chunks to eat while watching television; he'd eat them and then he'd do one of his unearthly belches and the den would reek of salami for the next fifteen minutes. Benjamin and Jeffrey also loved salami, but they, being children, couldn't be bothered to cut off slices, they'd merely go to the porch and take bites directly out of the hanging salami whenever they felt the urge. This gave the hanging salami a rather disgusting appearance but that mattered not one or two whits to the brothers Kritzer who would continue to bite away until the hanging salami was but a nub.

Given the Kritzers' love of food, it was only appropriate that Ernie Kritzer was a restaurateur. Ernie, over the years, had owned several fine restaurants, but for one reason or another most of them hadn't succeeded and he was down to one (not including several bars he owned), but that one was an unequivocal success.

The Erro was a wonderful steak house located near Western and Wilshire (on Serrano and 8th) and a stone's throw from downtown Los Angeles. Popular as both a lunch and dinner house, the Erro was frequented by successful businessmen at lunch, and swanky couples in the evening. The Erro was known for its prime steaks, fresh fish and giant Shrimp Cocktails. It was also known for Ernie's special steak sauce. Ernie had invented his special steak sauce because he simply thought that steak didn't taste like anything. He hated A1 Steak Sauce and hated Worcestershire Sauce even more. No, what Ernie Kritzer liked was ketchup. Plain and simple. Steak and ketchup. But he was smart enough to know that people wouldn't be caught dead using ketchup on a steak in a fancy restaurant. Ernie Kritzer's brilliant solution was to have his chef concoct a ketchup-based sauce (with a few herbs and spices added), which would then be put in a nice dish and served on the side. People loved that steak sauce and it was one of the reasons the restaurant was so popular.

Benjamin would accompany his father to the Erro during summer vacation, and he truly loved that restaurant. The chef (Al) and the barman (Jimmy or Angus, depending on the day) really liked Benjamin and they were all funny and gregarious. Ernie and Benjamin would arrive around ten in the morning. Ernie would go to his little office, which was located up some rickety stairs above the freezer where they kept all the meats and fish and Benjamin would go hang out with Al and Jimmy or Angus. Jimmy or Angus would pour him a Ginger Beer, and Benjamin would load it up with the maraschino cherries he so loved. Behind the bar was a huge Grundig Majestic World Radio that Benjamin would listen to while sipping his Ginger Beer and eating his cherries. The Grundig brought in stations from all over the world and Benjamin would twirl the dial and hear broadcasts from as far away as Germany, Sweden and England.

When it got closer to lunchtime, Benjamin would head into the kitchen, and there he'd eat some Shrimp Cocktail shrimp that were stored in a huge ice-filled barrel. His father had two kinds of cocktail sauce for dipping—a red sauce and a thousand island sauce—the latter is what Benjamin would use and he would just eat shrimp after shrimp, drowning each tasty morsel in the sauce. Al would watch him with amusement, and invariably Benjamin would glance over at Al with his mouth filled with shrimp, and in his best Grandpa Gelfinbaum voice would say, "What is it, fish?" which always made Al laugh even though he had no clue why Benjamin always said it.

Since his father didn't like him to be in the restaurant when the lunch patrons would arrive, Benjamin would vamoose from The Erro and go next door to Carl's Market. There he would kill time leafing through the magazines, which were housed in a rack in the liquor department. One day, while browsing through the latest *MAD* Magazine, Benjamin made an interesting discovery. At the very bottom of the magazine rack he noticed several magazines with bands around them. This intrigued him—what could be in those magazines that was so important that they put bands around them so people couldn't look through them? The magazines had titles like *Nude World*, *Nudist Life* and *Nude Living*.

Benjamin, surreptitiously checking to make sure the liquor man wasn't watching (he wasn't), knelt down, picked up *Nude Living* and put it behind his *MAD* Magazine. He then carefully removed the band and just as carefully began leafing through the magazine. In it were photographs of naked people doing things like lying on the grass or playing volleyball or just standing around laughing. Why were they all naked? Men, with their dinkles hanging there like so much fish, women with their boobies hanging there like so much fish, boys and girls with their miniature dinkles and girl parts (Benjamin wasn't sure what the girl part was called—he seemed to remember something along the lines of a Virginia, although that didn't seem right because certainly they would not name a girl part with the name of a state), all these naked people doing these activities without their clothes. Benjamin liked that magazine very much, especially the pictures with the girls. He wanted to buy that magazine but a) he didn't have the money, and b) the cover of the magazine loudly proclaimed "Adults Only". Benjamin thought this "Adults Only" business was ridiculous. After all, Ernie read Benjamin's comic books occasionally, and if an adult could read a kid's comic book then why couldn't a kid read an "Adults Only" magazine? It seemed so unfair, but what could eight-year-old Benjamin Kritzer do about it, sue someone? So, he had to be content to sneak whatever the latest "Nudist" magazine was under the latest *MAD* Magazine so that he could gaze longingly and lovingly at those cute little girls with their cute little girl Virginias.

CHAPTER FIVE
Words, Music,
and The Benjamin Kritzer Hour

Minnie Kritzer loved sayings. She used them whenever, wherever and however possible. Benjamin first heard one of Minnie's sayings one Christmas morning, when he'd opened a present from some relative or another, probably a pair of socks or underpants or something completely stupid that a child would never want as a gift and he'd tossed the present aside with Benjamin-like disdain. Minnie had immediately said, "Don't look a gift horse in the mouth." Benjamin looked at her for what seemed like days, scrunched up his face, and finally replied with an astonished, "*What?*" For weeks thereafter, Benjamin would ponder the meaning of "Don't look a gift horse in the mouth." And no matter how hard he pondered he could make no sense out of that sentence. Say someone actually gave you a horse as a gift. Why couldn't you look in its mouth? What would be so wrong in looking the gift horse in the mouth, if you were interested in things such as what the inside of the mouth of a horse looked like? When Benjamin finally asked his mother about it, she replied with her usual "Go play in traffic." When Benjamin informed her that he didn't want to go play in traffic, that he wanted to know what "Don't look a gift horse in the mouth" meant, Minnie Kritzer simply replied, "It's just a saying."

"Why?"

"Why? I don't know why. It's something people say. Don't make a mountain out of a molehill, Benjamin."

"How can you make a mountain out of a molehill?" asked Benjamin.

"Exactly," replied his mother.

If there had been any doubt whatsoever that his mother was a Martian, it was now completely gone.

"Do you make up these sayings?" Benjamin asked.

"Of course not. They're sayings."

"Who makes them up?"

"I don't know who makes them up, for God's sake. The saying people."

"The saying people?"

"Benjamin, you are giving me a migraine. Stop beating a dead horse."

Benjamin looked at the Martian who was his mother and then said, "I'm beating a dead horse? The gift horse? Why would anyone beat a dead gift horse? I don't get it."

"Benjamin, shut up. What is there to get? They're sayings, everyone says them."

"I've never heard anyone but you say them."

"Well now, that's a horse of a different color, isn't it? Besides, the proof is in the pudding." And with that Minnie Kritzer left the room.

Benjamin stood there, totally confused. The proof was in the pudding? He'd never seen anything in the pudding except the pudding (and occasionally whipped cream or milk). If the proof was somewhere it was *not* in the pudding, that much he knew. So, then, what was the point of the saying? And why were so many of these sayings about horses? He wanted to ask the saying people but he had no clue how to get hold of them.

This whole saying thing got him to thinking about words in general and spelling in general and sentences in general and language in general. One of the things he thought about was how you go from being a baby, saying goo-goo words and burbling through your drool, to talking. Where did those words suddenly come from and, more importantly, how did the baby suddenly know how to form those words into sentences and, more importantly, how did the baby even know what a sentence was, or what those words meant? It couldn't just be that the child heard the parents saying words and was suddenly able to interpret them and make coherent thoughts out of them, like "What is it, fish?" Where did the words *come* from? Who decided that there should be useless letters in words, like the "gh" in "thought" (not to mention the "u" and the "o"—just what *were* all those letters doing in there?). And if one were going to accept that all those useless letters should be in the word "thought", then who decided that they wouldn't be pronounced? Benjamin simply couldn't understand it. On the one hand you had a word like "though" and on the other hand you had a word like "thought". There was only a one-letter difference and yet they were pronounced totally differently. How arbitrary it all seemed. Somebody somewhere had made that decision about the pronunciation of "though" and "thought". Who? If there were saying people, were there word people? How, for example, had someone given the name "fish" to "fish"? Was there a man in olden times who suddenly looked at the creatures of the sea and thought, "I know, I'll call these things 'fish'"? Not to mention the various fish names like crab, shrimp, oysters and sturgeon. What kind of a mind made those names up, that's what Benjamin wanted to know. And why was a mop a mop and not a car? Why was a car a car and not a piano? Those word questions drove Benjamin crazy and he drove several of his teachers at Crescent Heights Elementary School crazy when he'd go on and on about the how, what, where and why of words. But if his teachers didn't have answers (they didn't), then who did?

***

In the summer of 1956, Benjamin's mother cashed in some S&H Green Stamps and got Benjamin an RCA 45rpm record player. It was a small compact little unit that played 45s, as you would imagine a 45rpm record player would. It was square-shaped and had a thick spindle onto which you could load a whole mess of 45s and they would plop down onto the turntable, one after another, song after song. Benjamin loved that record player and played it constantly. He would go over to the local record store, Index Radio and Records, on Shenandoah and Pico, and he'd buy all the latest 45s—Ricky Nelson, Elvis Presley, Chuck Berry, Fats Domino—if he'd saved enough allowance he might even splurge and get an EP, four songs instead of two and a picture cover to boot. That record player, to quote his mother, was the cat's pajamas, whatever *that* meant.

Sometimes, when Minnie was off playing Canasta and Benjamin was alone in the house, he'd take the record player into his mother's room, plug it in, and play his latest records. While doing that, he would take off all his clothes except his underwear and he'd then put on one of his mother's industrial strength girdles and brassieres. Benjamin was fascinated by those girdles and more fascinated with why anyone would wear such a contraption. He couldn't make sense of the little hook things used to attach the girdle to nylon stockings. Then again, he couldn't make sense of nylon stockings. But there he'd stand, in front of the closet mirror, wearing one of his mother's girdles and pointy brassieres, as *Hound Dog* or *Blueberry Hill* issued forth from the little record player. Benjamin would mime along with the song, as if he were Elvis Presley or Fats Domino, although he was pretty certain that Elvis or Fats didn't wear girdles and pointy brassieres when they performed.

Bruce Kimmel

Because there were jukeboxes in all of Ernie Kritzer's bars, Benjamin was lucky enough to get the castoff 45s that were removed to make room for the latest ones. So, Benjamin had quite a record collection to mime to.

The Kritzers also had the big hi-fi machine in the den, where you could play 78s and 33 1/3 LPs. Benjamin's favorites were the cast albums like *My Fair Lady*, *South Pacific* and *The King and I*. He could just listen to those for hours. The big hi-fi machine also had a very special feature—a record recorder. By placing the tone arm and needle toward the inside of the turntable onto a special blank Wilcox-Gay Recordio Disc and singing or speaking into the microphone, you could record your very own voice onto an actual record. The Kritzers made many lively recordings, including Ernie Kritzer reading to Benjamin and Jeffrey from various storybooks, and Minnie's ever-popular rendition of *My Yiddishe Mama*. That was Minnie's song and she would perform it anywhere at the drop of a hat, as she would put it. In fact, Minnie had wanted to be a singer (she had a pleasant if unmemorable voice, slightly on the nasal side), but that had all ended when she married Ernest Kritzer, because Ernest Kritzer didn't want a singer for a wife. Minnie resented this and would get back at Ernie by making endless recordings of *My Yiddishe Mama*. She sang it in English, she sang it in Yiddish, she sang it fast, she sang it slow, she sang it and sang it and sang it and then played those records over and over and over again and Benjamin heard them so many times that he began to pray that he'd be sucked up into the Hoover vacuum cleaner so he'd never have to hear it again. Other recordings included Ernie playing his violin (he had, at one time, played in a band, or so said those in the know—he'd given it up, though, because if Minnie couldn't be a singer, Ernie was most certainly not going to be a violin player), Jeffrey reciting the names of his favorite baseball players and their stats, and Benjamin singing his favorite songs like *Davy Crockett*, *Heartbreak Hotel*, and, of course, *When the Red Red Robin Comes Bob, Bob, Bobbin' Along*.

***

Given the success of his death scenes, his ability to mime while wearing a girdle and brassiere, and his many excellent homemade recordings, it was only natural that Benjamin would soon graduate to more sophisticated performing.

Every Monday night there would be a family dinner which would alternate between Minnie and Ernie's house, and Minnie's sister Lena and her husband Chaz's apartment, the upper half of a large duplex. Also attending would be Grandma and Grandpa Gelfinbaum, and occasionally an extra family member or two, such as cousin Yette and her daughter Rivka (and *her* daughter Karen), as well as Lena and Chaz's son and daughter, Denny and Dee Dee. Dinner would always consist of brisket (if at Minnie and Ernie's) or fried filet of sole and macaroni and cheese (if at Lena and Chaz's). This weekly event had been going on for as long as Benjamin could remember. After dinner, the women would retire to the kitchen to do the dishes and the men would light up their cigars and talk about the events of the day, while the kids would go in the den and argue about what TV show to watch. But, in 1956, all that changed because that was the premiere of The Benjamin Kritzer Hour.

From that point on, after dinner, dishes and cigars, Benjamin would corral everyone into the den where he would put on a weekly show for all attending relatives. They had no choice in whether they'd like to attend, attendance was mandatory and that was that. Sometimes his brother Jeffrey would insist on guest-starring in the show, much to Benjamin's chagrin, but Jeffrey was bigger and would threaten to put Benjamin's eye out if he couldn't guest star. This was not an idle threat because once Jeffrey had actually almost put out Benjamin's eye when, practicing his pitching, he'd asked Benjamin to be catcher; as he reared back, his fist had gone directly into Benjamin's eye—Benjamin had had to wear an eye patch for two weeks, during which time he looked like a weird child pirate.

In any case, the show would go on promptly at seven-thirty (it had to be finished in time for *I Love Lucy*) and the family would get a big kick out of it. Benjamin would mime *Hound Dog* (complete with all the proper Elvis moves, including gyrating pelvis) or *Blueberry Hill*, Jeffrey might play guitar (Jeffrey had gotten a guitar and could actually play four chords on it), and then Benjamin might do impressions of celebrities that he liked, such as Jack Benny (he had that deadpan look down to a "t", as his mother said—why he didn't have it down to an "s" or a "d" was something Minnie couldn't explain to him), and he did both Jackie Gleason *and* Art Carney in *The Honeymooners*. Of course, then Minnie would have to get up at everyone's insistence and do *My Yiddishe Mama* and sometimes Minnie, Lena and, horror of horrors, Grandma

Gelfinbaum, would do *Bei Mir Bist du Shoen* as if they were some totally demented Jewish version of The McGuire Sisters. The Benjamin Kritzer Hour was brought to you by Five Day Deodorant Pads (Benjamin did the commercials) and occasionally Prell Shampoo.

CHAPTER SIX

Autumn Leaves

August of 1956 brought rain to Los Angeles—not just a little rain but big huge buckets of rain. It rained every day for a solid week and Benjamin was in heaven because he loved rainy days, loved walking and running in the rain and even loved sitting inside by the window and watching it pour down, while he colored in his coloring books or read a Hardy Boys mystery.

Besides loving rain, Benjamin also loved Wednesdays, because a) that was the day the Kritzers' maid, Lulu (a big fat Black lady with a huge belly-laugh and great good humor) came and Benjamin loved Lulu (her full name was Lulu Salmon, and when Grandpa Gelfinbaum was introduced to her, he, of course, immediately said, "Lulu Salmon? What is it, fish?" and Lulu had howled with laughter like no one had ever made fun of her last name before), and b) Wednesday was the day when the movies changed and all the theaters would have brand new double bills. Benjamin would grab his father's *Herald Express* the minute he walked in the door after work, find the movie section, and spend the next half hour poring over the ads and the theater listings, deciding on what movies he would see that week.

***

Benjamin had awakened at nine on this particular Wednesday in this particularly rainy August, came into the kitchen and ate his usual breakfast (poached egg on toast and orange juice). Outside the window he could see the slate gray sky and the rain pouring down and hear it beating loudly on the roof. His mother said, "Just look at that rain. It's really coming down in sheets." Benjamin looked at her.

"It's coming down in sheets? How can rain come down in sheets?"

"What's the matter with you? Why do you have to question everything? It's just an expression, like it's raining cats and dogs."

"What does that *mean?*"

"It means it's raining hard."

"Then how come you don't say it's raining hard?"

"I *did* say it. I said it's coming down in sheets. I said it's raining cats and dogs. What is it that you don't understand, Benjamin? Why do you always have to be so weird?"

But Benjamin simply wanted to know how rain could come down in sheets and how it could rain cats and dogs. That wasn't weird, that was a perfectly normal thing for a person to wonder. What was weird was that some saying person would come up with such a stupid thing in the first place. He looked at his mother.

"Just answer me this. Why is it raining cats and dogs? Why isn't it raining elephants and zebras?"

Minnie looked at her son as if he were an open wound. "Benjamin, let sleeping dogs lie," and with that she went back to washing the breakfast dishes. Benjamin scratched his head.

"I should let a sleeping dog lie? How can a dog lie if it's sleeping? Why would a dog tell a lie in the first place?"

Minnie wheeled around and yelled at Benjamin. "Lie, as in lie on the ground, not lie as in tell a lie."

And that was another thing: Why were there words that had two meanings? Lie and lie, for example. Whose bright idea was *that*?

"I'm just trying to…"

"Benjamin, you are really getting my goat."

Now he was getting her goat? His mother had a goat? And he was getting it? And sleeping dogs were telling lies and rain was coming down in sheets like cats and dogs and Benjamin was just not ever going to understand this word business, that much was clear.

Ernie arrived home at four-thirty, *Herald Express* in hand. It was still raining cats and dogs and coming down in sheets and Ernie was soaked. While he went to get in his pajama top, Benjamin took the movie section and began perusing the theater listings. The new show at the Lido was the one he wanted to see—Alfred Hitchcock's *The Man Who Knew Too Much*, playing with something called *Autumn Leaves*. Benjamin loved *Alfred Hitchcock Presents* on television, loved the roly-poly Englishman and his funny introductions and funny putdowns of the commercials. He'd seen *To Catch A Thief* the year before and loved every minute of it, so he was most anxious to see *The Man Who Knew Too Much*. Jeffrey wanted to see it too, so the two of them would go together. The show started at six-thirty, so if they left by five-thirty that would give them enough time to stop at Kentucky Boys, the little diner on the corner of Sherbourne and Pico (across from Leo's Delicatessen) for a hamburger (Benjamin's favorite hamburger) and fries before heading over to the Lido which was a block and a half from there. Minnie made Benjamin put on his bright yellow raincoat and his bright yellow galoshes. How anyone could name a pair of rain shoes "galoshes" was beyond him. Someone somewhere had actually looked at those protective overshoes and thought, "What should I name these? I know—galoshes!" Or, maybe the inventor of those overshoes was named Herman Galoshes; at least that would make sense. Oh, well, Benjamin didn't have time to ponder the mystery of the galoshes and he knew if he brought it up to his mother that he would never make the movie in time, so he let sleeping dogs lie.

After finishing their delicious Kentucky Boys burgers (truth be told, in a rare show of brotherly emotion, Jeffrey ate there even though he detested the greasy burgers, because he knew Benjamin loved them), they ran the block and a half to the Lido in the rain. As they approached the theater, Benjamin saw the marquee (now lit up in all its bright Technicolor neon glory), which had the new double bill up in bright red letters. They bought their fifteen-cent tickets, but before they could go in, Benjamin, as was his wont, had to examine all the posters for the upcoming films. Once inside, Jeffrey bought his favorite candy, Jujubes, and Benjamin bought a Charms sucker, not his favorite but it was cheap and lasted forever, and a frozen U-No Bar. Jeffrey would always wonder why Benjamin liked those dopey frozen U-No Bars—Jeffrey thought they tasted like chalk—and when he'd ask Benjamin why he liked the U-No so much, Benjamin would always open his eyes wide and reply in his scariest voice, "You know."

They entered the auditorium in which there were maybe fifty other people. Benjamin went directly to his tenth row aisle seat (woe to anyone who'd make the mistake of already being seated there—if that were the case then Benjamin would sit behind whoever the inconsiderate oaf was and he would make unseemly loud fart noises until the inconsiderate oaf invariably moved—then Benjamin immediately moved once again to his personal seat), and Jeffrey went to the front row where he liked to sit.

The lights dimmed, the curtains opened and the first feature came on, which was *Autumn Leaves*. Benjamin read the credits carefully as he always did, noting that it starred Joan Crawford and Cliff Robertson and was in black and white. *Autumn Leaves* was a little turgid for Benjamin, but he sat there attentively following its story as best he could. He followed it until the scene in which Cliff Robertson threw a typewriter on Joan Crawford's hand. Joan's scream and the viciousness of the throwing of the typewriter on her hand sent Benjamin directly up the aisle to the lobby. That scene just disturbed his little eight-year-old sensibilities, and he was quite upset that someone would throw a typewriter on poor Joan Crawford's hand. Benjamin went up the stairs and went into the men's room. He didn't really have to go, so he just looked around, flushed all the toilets, and left.

As he was walking to the stairs he noticed a door across from where the bathrooms were located. The door was slightly open and Benjamin could hear the sound of the movie coming faintly from behind it. He wandered over to it and peeked in. His eyes widened as he saw two giant projectors, one of which was running loudly. In front of the projectors were little glass portholes and the beam of light from the running projector made a miniature version of the film image on the glass. Benjamin was mesmerized. He'd often looked up toward those little portholes when he was in the auditorium, following the huge shaft of light to the upper back wall from where the light emanated. He'd seen those little miniature-looking images on the glass, but for some reason he'd always assumed that someone was up there watching a small television.

The projector made quite a bit of noise as the reel spun around and around. Benjamin then noticed the man in the booth was putting up a reel and feeding the film into the projector not in use. The man suddenly became aware of Benjamin peeking through the door. He turned his head, smiled and said, "Hi there. Don't care for the movie?" Benjamin told the man that he didn't like when crazy Cliff Robertson threw the typewriter on nice Joan Crawford's hand, and the man shook his head in agreement and said, "I know what you mean." Benjamin, eyes still wide, asked, "What do you do in here?" The man gestured for him to come in, which Benjamin happily did.

"This is where we show the movies from. These are projectors and these are the reels of film. See, I'm loading up this projector now so that when that projector over there finishes the reel of film that's on it, I start this one up and it takes over. Did you know that it takes two projectors to show a movie?"

Benjamin had noticed (when he became bored with a movie) that when he'd look up to where the shaft of light was coming from that it would always alternate between two portholes. Now he knew why—two projectors to show a movie. The man beckoned Benjamin closer.

"Now, watch this—here's something I'll bet you never noticed before. You might wonder how I know when to start up the second projector. Well, it's simple." The man got a wooden box and put it on the floor in front of a window that was next to the projector.

"Stand up here now and look out the window," the man said. Benjamin did so and through the window he could see the movie being shown on the screen downstairs.

"Okay, now, see how the reel of film on that projector over there is almost to the end? In a minute you're going to hear a bell, and when you hear that bell I want you to watch the movie screen very carefully."

Benjamin listened, and sure enough about twenty seconds later he heard a little bell sound in the room. The man put his hand on a lever on the projector and then said, "Okay, now watch the very very top right-hand side of the screen. Can you see it?" Benjamin said he could. The man continued, "In about thirty seconds you're going to see a circle, like a big dot, up there, and then in a few seconds you'll see another one. When the first one appears, that's when I'm going to pull this lever here, and this projector will start running. When the second dot appears a little shutter goes down and shuts off the picture on that projector and at the same time this projector lights up and starts showing this reel at exactly the point where the other reel left off. Now, watch."

Benjamin stared as hard as he could at the very very top of the right-hand side of the screen, and by golly if he didn't see the first dot up there. The man pulled the lever and the projector whirled into motion. In a moment, the second dot appeared and suddenly the projector that Benjamin was next to was throwing the beam of light onto its glass. Benjamin looked over to the other projector and there was no light being thrown from there anymore and it was shutting off. It was one of the most amazing things Benjamin had ever seen in his life. There must have been a look of extreme astonishment on Benjamin's face, because the man was laughing and saying, "Pretty interesting, huh?" Interesting wasn't the word, interesting simply didn't describe what Benjamin Kritzer had just seen. The man let Benjamin stay in the room for the duration of *Autumn Leaves* and Benjamin saw him do two more of what the man called "changeovers". Benjamin couldn't wait to amaze and impress everyone he knew with his knowledge of the dots and What They Meant. At the end of *Autumn Leaves*, Benjamin thanked the man, left the booth feeling very elated, rolled down the stairs and went back into the auditorium. He found Jeffrey and told him of his magical adventure in the projection booth. Naturally, Jeffrey believed him not one or even two whits.

Then came the main feature, *The Man Who Knew Too Much*, which Benjamin thought was great. From the opening Paramount and

VistaVision logos, to the pulse-pounding music (he even made a mental note of the composer's name, Bernard Herrmann) to the exotic locales (Marrakech and London), Benjamin savored every minute. He totally identified with the little boy who was kidnapped, and he totally wished he could have Doris Day and James Stewart as parents. He loved the song that Doris Day sang to her son, *Que Será Será (Whatever Will Be, Will Be)* and thought it would be ever so much nicer to have a mother sing that song instead of one who sang *My Yiddishe Mama* all the time. His favorite scene was the one where someone got stabbed in the back and went through the Marrakech marketplace not being able to quite reach the knife to pull it out. Benjamin loved that scene, and for some days thereafter he would imitate that scene all over the house.

The following day he hurried over to Index Records and Radio and bought the 45 of *Que Será Será*, which he played and played and played until it was worn out. All around the house Benjamin could be heard singing loudly

"Que será será
Whatever will be will be
The future's not ours to see
Que será será
What will be will be."

He sang it so much that Minnie finally looked at him and said, "I'll tell you what will be will be—if you don't shut up with that song already, you will not get any dessert tonight." Since Benjamin had already visited both the Helms Man and the Good Humor Man that day, the no dessert business was hardly a threat, so he continued singing at the top of his lungs

"When I was just a little girl
I asked my mother what will I be?
Will I be pretty, will I be rich?
Here's what she said to me
Que será será!"

until Minnie finally screamed at him, "Benjamin, shut up or I'm going to brain you." That shut Benjamin right up because he was trying to figure out how you "brain" someone. He started to laugh because he suddenly had an image of his mother smacking him with a brain.

"What are you laughing at?"

"You braining me."

"You won't think it's so funny when I brain you, wise guy."

Benjamin started singing again

"Que será será
Whatever will be will be"

which finally drove Minnie to her bedroom where she had to lie down (like a sleeping dog) and give herself the Witch Hazel pad treatment.

Bruce Kimmel

CHAPTER SEVEN
Crescent Heights, Girls in Their Underpants and Warts

Benjamin hadn't liked any of his teachers prior to Mrs. Wallett. Mrs. Wallett taught fourth grade at Crescent Heights Elementary School, and she was, Benjamin thought, friendly and nice and she seemed to actually take an interest in her students and didn't do what his teachers before her had done—inundate the students with busy work and homework. In fact, the only thing Benjamin really liked about school prior to the fourth grade and Mrs. Wallett were girls. He'd already come to this realization: While all the other boys just wanted to hang around each other and make fun of girls, all Benjamin wanted to do was be with girls and never hang around boys. He hated boys. He supposed he'd always felt that way, but now it was really clear to him. He *hated* boys and loved girls.

He didn't want to do any of the normal boy things; he didn't want to play baseball, football, basketball, volleyball, tetherball, kickball or any other ball. He didn't want to throw a shot put like his brother. He didn't want to play "war" or "cowboys and Indians" (although he did have his Fanner 50 and a Wild Bill Hickock rifle) or any other boy games. No, what Benjamin Kritzer wanted was to be around girls, to look at them, to hold their hands, to look up their dresses and see their underpants. He achieved the latter by simply lying on the school ground pavement as if he'd fallen and when the girls would pass by or stop to see what was wrong he'd get an eyeful of those beautiful underpants. Oh, how he loved girls in their underpants. But not just any underpants, no, Benjamin was very particular about underpants. Benjamin liked *cotton* underpants and only cotton underpants and if a girl were wearing any other kind of underpants then those girls were of no interest to him. Plain white were his favorite, but he also liked pink and yellow and blue and purple and ones with flowers on them and ones with polka dots on them and ones with stripes on them. He knew this was strange for an eight-year-old grammar school child—this obsession with girls in their underpants. It just wasn't The Way Things Were—boys stuck with boys and made fun of girls, and girls stuck with girls and giggled at the boys who were making fun of them.

He kept a list in his notebook of the girls whose underpants he'd seen—Rachel Sperber, Ellen Gelman, Cynthia Tidings, Leah Holtzman, and Brenda Cohen were a few of the names in his notebook, and the list grew daily. Of course, nowhere in the notebook were the names of girls who didn't wear cotton underpants. There was simply no room for those girls who wore nylon underpants, or, even worse, nylon underpants with little frilly doo-dads all over them like Francine Lentner for example. Benjamin had once been looking up her dress and not only was she wearing the dreaded nylon underpants with the dreaded frilly doo-dads, those nylon underpants with the frilly doo-dads had "Wednesday" written on them. As if that weren't bad enough, she was wearing the "Wednesday" underpants on Friday. Wasn't that just typical of someone who wore nylon underpants?

Other than girls in their underpants, school was a chore for Benjamin. He would much rather have been at home, watching Sheriff John or playing miniature golf or fooling around on the Adohr trucks, than having to endure things that he had no interest in whatsoever, things like history and math and geography. He did like reading, and he was an excellent speller and always won the spelling bees.

The one school thing Benjamin did look forward to was field trips. He'd been to the planetarium, he'd been to the San Fernando Mission, and he'd been to the Museum of Natural History. Benjamin loved those field trips; it was like getting out of school for the day as far as he was concerned. He loved them until, that is, one fateful day in October of 1956 when Mrs. Wallett took the class on a field trip to a tuna-canning factory.

All the kids in Mrs. Wallett's fourth grade class had had their permission slips signed, and they were herded into the bright yellow school bus and then driven to San Pedro, where the tuna-canning factory was located. Once there, the kids exited the bus, got in line, and were taken to the entrance of the tuna-canning factory, where they were met by the tuna-canning factory guide. They were then led into the facility and the tour began. First they were shown the place where all the dead tuna were taken to be tunaized or whatever they did to tuna to make it look like the stuff that ended up in the cans. There were thousands of dead tuna there (Grandpa Gelfinbaum would have *loved* this place—"What is it, fish?" he would have said immediately), and the class was suitably impressed. Benjamin was not suitably impressed, however. What Benjamin was was nauseous. Not only was he nauseous, his face had turned a bilious shade of green (rather like the swan wallpaper in his dining room). His nausea and bilious green shade were caused by the smell of the dead tuna which had wafted its way into his nostrils with the force of a tidal wave, and that smell was horrendous, that smell was stultifying, that smell was simply the worst smell Benjamin Kritzer had ever smelled in all his eight years. It was the smell of dead tuna. *Really* dead tuna. Tuna that was no longer living. Thousands of tuna lying there without a care in the world because they were dead. Couldn't be deader than these tuna, Benjamin thought. The nausea he was feeling was growing and he felt as if he were going to vomit right there all over the dead tuna. Funnily enough, the other kids didn't even seem to be taking notice of the dead tuna smell because they were busy oohing and ahhing and being amazed at so many dead tuna in one place at one time. Benjamin looked for Mrs. Wallett, to tell her he needed to be outside, that he needed to breathe some non-dead tuna air, but Mrs. Wallett, clever woman that she was, was nowhere to be found.

Benjamin went up to the tour guide and asked him if he could please go outside because he was feeling sick to his stomach on account of the dead tuna smell. The tour guide told him to hold on, that they were going to the canning department and that the tour would be over soon. Benjamin went back to his schoolmates and they were then taken to the part of the factory where the actual canning took place. Benjamin was turning greener by the minute and he felt something that didn't taste very good coming up in his throat. He didn't really want to vomit in front of everyone because while Benjamin liked the *word* vomit, he hated the actual *act* of vomiting and had, in fact, vowed never to vomit again. But the dead tuna smell was taxing his ability to keep that vow and taxing it heavily. He tried to think of other things, tried to get his mind off the smell of the dead tuna. He thought of the smell of roses (his favorite flower smell), he thought of the smell of a Helms chocolate donut (his favorite food smell), he thought of the smell of a freshly peeled orange (his favorite fruit smell), but no matter what he thought of, he still smelled the dead tuna. Finally, about ten minutes later (it seemed like hours to Benjamin) the tour was over and the kids were taken outside. Benjamin breathed in the fresh air in great big gulps and gradually his green hue began to return to a normal color. The bus ride back to school made his nausea worse, but he made it without vomiting and by the time he got home the nausea had abated somewhat. But he couldn't get that dead tuna smell out of his mind and even though he was miles and miles away from it he still smelled it as if it were right there in the room with him.

Benjamin still smelled the dead tuna smell when he woke up the next morning, and he smelled it on his way to school and he smelled it in Mrs. Wallett's classroom. It was everywhere, the smell of dead tuna. At lunch, the smell had finally begun to go away. Benjamin was sitting on a bench in the lunch court and opened his brown paper sack lunch (with Benjamin Kritzer written on the front) and pulled out his Saran-wrapped sandwich. It was a tuna sandwich. He could not believe it. A smelly dead tuna sandwich. He wanted to brain his mother right then and there but he didn't have a spare brain lying around. He rewrapped the smelly dead tuna sandwich and then promptly dropped it into the nearest trashcan.

***

Then came the curious episode of the warts. One day Benjamin awoke to find a peculiar bump on his right palm. He thought nothing of it, but over the next few days he was alarmed to see it grow into a rather large and ugly peculiar bump that resembled, of all things, the candy found in a box of Dots. He showed it to his mother who looked at it and said, "That's a wart. How did you get a wart?"

"How did I get a wart? I don't know how I got a wart. It just showed up."

"Well, we're going to have to go to the doctor right now so he can cut it off."

Benjamin did not like the sound of that at all. But Minnie called the family doctor and off they went an hour later.

Doctor Hallberg said, "Strip down to your underwear." Benjamin didn't like stripping down to his underwear, not in front of a stranger, and not even in front of his parents or his brother. Benjamin would usually dress and undress in the closet. Besides, why did he have to strip down to his underwear when the wart was on his hand? In any case, Benjamin did as he was told. The doctor tapped his chest, tapped his back, listened to his heart through a cold metal stethoscope, and looked in his ear with that ear thing which Benjamin didn't know the name of. As he was poked and listened to, Benjamin wondered why a stethoscope was called a stethoscope, which, to him, rather sounded like Cinemascope. See all the wonders of the screen in thrilling Stethoscope. Finally, the doctor looked at Benjamin's hand. He studied it for a moment and then proclaimed, "What we have here is a wart." He explained that warts were a tumorous growth usually caused by a viral infection. All this went directly over Benjamin's head because as Doctor Hallberg was saying all this Benjamin watched with ever-growing nervousness as the nurse prepared a huge syringe. When he saw that huge syringe, Benjamin knew he was going to get a shot and Benjamin did not like shots, couldn't stand shots, shots were right up there with milk en vasser and head cheese in the Benjamin Kritzer hatred department. The doctor was saying something about lancing but all Benjamin could see was that syringe and the big needle attached to it.

"I'm going to give you a local anesthetic, Benjamin, so that when I lance the wart off it won't hurt at all."

The nurse handed the syringe to Doctor Hallberg. Benjamin thought of running from the room, running from the doctor's office, running down the street to safety, but he was in his underwear so what could he do but sit there and let this doctor give him whatever a local anesthetic was. The doctor took Benjamin's hand and without any warning just stuck that big needle right in next to where the wart was. The doctor wiggled the needle around and injected the contents of the syringe into Benjamin's hand. Benjamin thought about crying because, as his mother liked to say (when she had a corn or a bunion), it hurt like the dickens (he had no idea what a dickens was, but if this hurt like it he felt very sorry for the dickens), but Benjamin would not cry, his crying days were long gone. The doctor finally removed the needle from Benjamin's hand. Within minutes Benjamin's hand had no feeling in it whatsoever. It was totally numb. The nurse then gave the doctor a scalpel. The doctor then asked Benjamin to lie down on the table and suggested he close his eyes. Benjamin did as he was told. As he lay there with eyes closed, he could feel a little tingling sensation on his hand, and he could hear scraping sounds. He wished he could fall asleep so he wouldn't have to hear the scraping sounds, but he just lay there (let sleeping Benjamins lie, his mother would probably say). A little while later, the doctor told him he could open his eyes and sit up. Benjamin sat up and looked at his hand, which was now bandaged.

"There you go," the doctor said. "No more wart. That wasn't too bad, was it?"

Well, Benjamin supposed, it depended on your definition of "bad". Benjamin decided that someone putting a big needle in your hand next to a wart was definitely in the bad category. So, he ignored the question and put his clothes back on. The doctor patted him on the head and told him to take a lollipop on his way out. Benjamin thought a lollipop was hardly enough reward for enduring the needle in the hand, so Minnie took Benjamin to Ralph's Five and Dime and let him buy whatever he wanted. He chose a new coloring book (he knew he was too old for coloring books, but he loved them just the same) and a spud gun so that in case the Bad Men made a sudden appearance he could shoot them with a potato.

When they got home that afternoon, Minnie went directly to the refrigerator and got out an apple, which she thrust at Benjamin.

"Eat this."

"I'm not hungry."

"Eat it anyway. Now."

"Why?"

"Because you have to eat an apple and then we have to bury the core wrapped in a handkerchief in the backyard. That way you'll never have another wart again."

Benjamin realized that there was no arguing with a person who would believe that an apple core wrapped in a handkerchief buried in the backyard would somehow prevent warts from returning, so he ate the apple; then Minnie duly wrapped the core in a handkerchief and the two of them went out back and buried it in the dirt near the incinerator.

Funnily, Benjamin never had another wart.

CHAPTER EIGHT
The Chop-o-Matic,
and Benjamin in the Bathroom

Sometime in October of 1956, Benjamin discovered the joys of mail order. He loved looking at the tiny ads in the occasional *Superman* comic book he bought, or in the *National Geographic* magazines that his father would bring home (not that Ernie ever read *National Geographic*, but he did like the way it looked on the coffee table—no, Ernie's tastes ran to Perry Mason books and lurid *True Detective* magazines, which, of course, had the best tiny ads of all), and he loved the ads on television where you could call and order things that would be sent directly to your very own house. At eight years of age, Benjamin decided that he loved getting things in the mail. So, he began sending away for any and everything that was free—catalogs, samples, trial issues of magazines—whatever he could get for the cost of a stamp, he'd get. Every day when he'd get home from school he'd run to the mailbox to see what was there (or, if the mail had already been taken out, Benjamin would shove his hand up the slot because frequently mail would become stuck on the way down), and he was giddy every time there was an envelope for him. He pored over his catalogs and magazines and displayed whatever samples he got. He got lots and lots of maps—it seemed everyone wanted to send maps and Benjamin, despite his complete disinterest in geography, loved looking at the maps from all over the country. He liked the colors and the shapes of the states and cities and the lines that represented roads and highways. He amassed quite a collection—nothing to rival his collection of bottle caps, but quite a collection nonetheless.

One day he was watching *Mr. District Attorney* on television and an ad came on for something called a Chop-o-Matic. The Chop-o-Matic was a handy-dandy device into which you'd put an onion, for example, and then by pressing the handy-dandy lever you'd chop that onion into neat little onion bits. No more onion tears, said the ad, and you could chop celery and carrots and radishes and all manner of vegetables and things. Best of all, by calling the handy-dandy phone number on the screen you could order the Chop-o-Matic and for a very reasonable price it would be sent directly to your house. Benjamin wanted that Chop-o-Matic but he knew if he went to his mother that she'd just say "Go play in traffic" and not understand at all that she would never again have onion tears. The Chop-o-Matic spokesperson went on to say that you didn't even have to send money, you could order it COD. That sounded very good to Benjamin—you could order it and you didn't have to send money. He didn't really know what COD was (except that it spelled "cod" which was one of Grandpa Gelfinbaum's favorite what-is-it-fish fishes), but Benjamin knew a good deal when he heard one. "Send no money, just call the toll-free number and we'll send you the Chop-o-Matic COD." So, Benjamin called the toll-free number and ordered the Chop-o-Matic COD. He then totally forgot about it, because he was busy sending away for novelty items (for $1.00 you could get ten novelty items—very exciting), carefully enclosing his one-dollar allowance in an envelope and mailing it at the corner mailbox on his way to school.

A week later, Benjamin arrived home to find his mother glaring at him with "that" look. The wooden hanger look. In her hand was a box which she was tapping with the fingernails on her other hand. Tapping furiously.

"Well?" Tap. Tap. Tap.

"Well what?"

"Well, what do you have to say for yourself?"

"I'm home?"

"No, that is not the right answer. That answer, Benjamin, will not cut the mustard, if you get my meaning."

Benjamin wondered how his answer could cut the mustard, but he could come up with no logical explanation. In fact, he couldn't think of anything that *would* cut the mustard. Or the ketchup for that matter. How could you cut mustard and why would you want to? He obviously was not getting his mother's meaning, but rather than mention that fact to someone who had the hanger look in her eyes, Benjamin let it pass.

"This package arrived today, Benjamin," his mother said ominously. "This package arrived COD. I had to pay for this package which you, Benjamin, apparently ordered."

It all finally came clear to Benjamin. "The Chop-o-Matic?"

Minnie turned the box around so that it faced Benjamin. There, on the front of the box was an image of the Chop-o-Matic. "Yes, the Chop-o-Matic. The nineteen-dollar-and-ninety-five cent Chop-o-Matic. Why did you order this thing, Benjamin?"

"So you wouldn't have any more onion tears. The ad said no more onion tears."

"You were worried about my onion tears? What did I do to deserve such an idiot for a child?"

"I thought you'd like it. It's really easy to use and you can chop vegetables in seconds."

"What are you, a commercial? I'm not the one who'll be chopping vegetables in seconds. First of all, I'm taking one dollar out of your allowance every week until this is paid for. What do you think about that?"

"I only *get* a dollar."

"Not for the next twenty weeks you don't. Furthermore, you are now in charge of all vegetable chopping. You'll learn to use this machine and you will chop all vegetables that need chopping and that's all there is to it." Before Benjamin could even open his mouth to speak, Minnie added, "Don't argue with me, Benjamin." With that, she thrust the box into his hands and stormed out of the room.

He wasn't too upset about the no allowance for twenty weeks business. She'd made that threat before and then quickly forgotten it. He took the box into the kitchen, opened it and pulled out the Chop-o-Matic. It didn't look quite as sturdy as the one on television, but Benjamin was very excited to have his very own Chop-o-Matic, even if it was a little rickety. He was quite certain that the other boys on the block didn't have their very own Chop-o-Matic, not Paul Needle (too busy sucking eggs), not Tommy Line, not Michael Krieger, not any of them. His mother thought that having to use the Chop-o-Matic was punishment? Hah, thought Benjamin, all punishment should be like that. He went to the refrigerator, pulled out an onion, took it over to the machine and placed it under the plastic hood. He pressed down on the lever with all his eight-year-old might. But the blades didn't penetrate very far into the onion. He lifted the machine and disengaged the onion from the blades. He then pushed the lever again with even more of his eight-year-old might. Nothing. He lifted the machine again, disengaged the onion again and tried again. But the blades would not cut through the onion, hence he could not chop the onion, hence, to use his mother's expression, this machine was not cutting the mustard *or* the onion. He got a knife from the drawer and carefully diced the onion and then put the results under the plastic hood of the machine. In the nick of time, too, as Minnie had just come back to the kitchen. She looked at the chopped onion under the hood of the machine, and then at

Benjamin whose eyes were quite red and filled with onion tears (the only kind he would cry).

"Well, I guess the 'no onion tears' was a bunch of baloney, huh? Still, it did do a nice job of chopping the onion. Well, I guess I'll make your father's favorite hamburgers tonight, as long as the onion's chopped."

Benjamin liked watching her make those hideous-looking hamburgers; she'd mush together the raw hamburger meat with onions and eggs and ketchup and form the resultant glop into little lumps that she amusingly called "hamburgers". Certainly they did not resemble the hamburgers that Benjamin got at Kentucky Boys or Fosters Freeze. These "hamburgers" were then ceremoniously dumped on the plate, without buns, and eaten with lots and lots and lots of Heinz 57 Ketchup. The leftovers were put in the refrigerator where the grease would congeal into a crusty white mass, which, of course, didn't stop Ernie Kritzer from finishing them later that night while watching television.

The Chop-o-Matic did manage to do okay on celery and carrots and Benjamin liked watching the blades chop those vegetables into semi-neat little cubes. His mother did indeed forget to take the one and only dollar from his allowance, and she even used the Chop-o-Matic once or twice herself (although she didn't tell Benjamin about it).

***

A few weeks later, Benjamin's ten novelty items arrived (luckily he retrieved them from the mailbox before his mother did). He secreted the box to his bedroom, ripped it open and took out the ten novelty items. They were fantastic, these novelty items and well worth the dollar Benjamin had paid for them. Plus, there was a catalog for 3,001 *more* novelty items, which is why, Benjamin guessed, they gave you the first ten for a dollar. Get you hooked and then you *had* to buy more. He spread the ten novelty items out on his bed and checked out each one very carefully. He especially liked the fake vomit and the plastic dog poop. The dismembered bloody finger was nice, the glow in the dark miniature skeleton head was fine too, but the rest were pretty lame, Benjamin thought, especially the X-Ray Specks and the Sea Monkeys. The X-Ray Specks were just cardboard glasses with little pinholes for the eyes, and in no way could you see under people's clothing as promised. Benjamin knew that for a fact because he'd worn the X-Ray Specks to school in hopes of seeing right through all the girls' dresses directly to their underpants, and he was mightily disappointed that he couldn't. Not only that, but he looked totally ridiculous in the glasses and was the object of much derision from his schoolmates. As to the Sea Monkeys, he put one in water and it just lay there like so much fish, doing absolutely nothing. Frankly, it didn't even resemble a monkey so what the point of the Sea Monkey was Benjamin couldn't fathom.

Lulu Salmon was the first to find the fake vomit, which Benjamin had placed on the floor near his bed on cleaning day. She shrieked when she saw it, then looked closer only to find it was made out of rubber. Benjamin, who'd been hiding in his closet, howled with laughter, and when she heard him howling, Lulu joined right in, bellowing her infectious laugh.

"Lordy, what will they think of next?"

"This," said Benjamin, and thrust the fake dog poop at her.

"You stay away from me with that, that is disgusting!"

She ran from the room, and Benjamin could hear her laughter bellowing all the way down the hall.

Later that day, while Lulu was ironing, Benjamin was in the kitchen using the Chop-o-Matic. He suddenly screamed loudly and Lulu came running in. Benjamin was standing at the sink, the Chop-o-Matic in front of him, and he pointed at it.

"I cut off my finger," Benjamin wailed dramatically, and when Lulu looked closer, she saw the bloody dismembered finger sitting under the plastic hood of the Chop-o-Matic, mixed in with the celery. By that time Benjamin had fallen on the floor, convulsed with laughter. He was laughing so hard he could barely breathe and tears were streaming down his face.

"I am gonna whup you, you little devil," Lulu howled. "Your little *be*hind is gonna be redder than a radish." Benjamin got up quickly and ran, still laughing, as Lulu chased him around the house, laughing as hard as Benjamin was.

Late at night he'd study his 3,001 Novelty Items catalog, reading each and every ad, making little check marks next to things he felt he had to have, although he never did get around to ordering anything else.

***

Benjamin's favorite nighttime activity (besides watching his favorite television shows) was locking himself in his parents' bathroom for his nightly shower. He'd be in there for over an hour, although only five minutes of that hour was actually used for showering. The other fifty-five minutes were taken up with Benjamin going through the drawers and the medicine cabinet and having fun with what he found therein. He liked to draw a moustache on with his mother's eyebrow pencil, and he liked putting on his mother's lipstick and his father's shaving cream all over his face. He looked a sight, Benjamin did, what with his moustache and ruby red lips and shaving cream. He studied the packages that contained treatments for bunions and corns, opened all the jars of cold creams and ointments so he could smell and occasionally try them, put Minnie's curlers in his hair (as best he could—he didn't quite get the hang of how the curlers actually worked) and checked out her endless supply of Five Day Deodorant Pads. Benjamin thought those pads were hilarious. They were small and round and had a useless hole in the middle and they stunk to high heaven and Benjamin liked putting them on his forehead. He thought that was endlessly amusing, looking at himself in the mirror with a Five Day Deodorant Pad stuck on his forehead.

Eventually there would be a pounding on the door, followed by Minnie yelling, "What are you *doing* in there, for God's sake? Open the door this minute." "I'm coming," Benjamin would yell back, and then he'd have to scurry and put everything back, then jump in the shower to wash all the guck off. He'd come out of the bathroom all squeaky clean

Bruce Kimmel

in his pajamas and no one was ever the wiser to his bathroom activities, although Minnie's supply of Five Day Deodorant Pads did seem to be dwindling awfully fast.

CHAPTER NINE
Foreign Intrigue

Towards the end of 1956, just before Benjamin's ninth birthday and during the school holiday break, the Kritzers took a family vacation. They went to a jolly seaside community called La Jolla and stayed at a very nice hotel. Two important events happened on that trip. The first event happened in the early evening of their second day at the hotel. His parents had gone off to dine in the hotel restaurant with some of their friends. Somehow, Benjamin had been playing with the window—one of those where you turned a knob and the window went either out or back in—and somehow while turning the knob back and forth, causing the window to go in and out, he'd banged his forehead on the metal tip of the bottom of the window. This created a nice ugly gash on Benjamin's forehead and it was quite painful not to mention quite bloody. He and his brother ran to the restaurant to tell his parents.

His mother took one look at the gash and said, "What can you do with such a child?" while his father got up from the table, grabbed Benjamin by the arm, took him outside and promptly slapped him across the face, yelling, "Why do you always have to ruin everything?" He was taken back to the room, some first aid (iodine) and a bandage was applied, and then his father went back to finish his dinner (nothing could stop Ernie Kritzer from finishing his dinner). Benjamin felt bad that he apparently always had to ruin everything, but he found that the really interesting thing was that when his father had slapped him across the face, the pain of the gash no longer bothered him because the pain was much worse in his cheek. He called this rather interesting discovery "redirecting the pain" and it always worked. If, for example, one of his idiot friends was complaining that his tooth ached, Benjamin would kick the friend really hard in the shin. The friend, usually with a shocked expression, would look at Benjamin and cry out, "What did you do that for?" to which Benjamin would simply reply, "I'm redirecting the pain." And, of course, while the idiot boy was rubbing his aching shin, damned if he hadn't forgotten all about his aching tooth.

The second important event happened when Minnie dropped Benjamin off at a nearby La Jolla movie theater to see the early evening show. The main feature was called *Foreign Intrigue* and it starred Robert Mitchum. It was indeed a story of foreign intrigue, with people double-crossing people and lots of shadowy streets in faraway countries. Benjamin liked these sorts of movies, with spies and villains and mysterious goings-on. But it was about halfway through the movie that Benjamin sat up in his tenth row seat, sat up and could not take his eyes from the screen. That was because a stunningly beautiful blonde girl had suddenly appeared. She was foreign and Benjamin was intrigued because she was just about the most beautiful person he'd ever seen. She was blonde, about twenty Benjamin guessed, and something about her caused him to fall head over heels in love right then and there. He sat, eyes riveted, whenever she was on the screen.

After the film ended he sat through the second feature but had no idea what it was, who was in it, or what it was about, because all he could think of was the girl from *Foreign Intrigue*. He left the theater almost in a trance. He didn't even use the men's room or roll down the stairs.

Minnie was waiting for him in front of the theater, but before he got in the car, he made sure to look at the poster to find out the beautiful girl's name. There were two female names on the poster—Genevieve Page was the first, but Benjamin was absolutely certain that she'd played the bad lady. No, the minute he saw the other name he knew it was her, because the name was as alluring as she was—Ingrid Tulean. He was brought out of his trance by Minnie honking the Oldsmobile's horn. Benjamin got in the car and they headed back to the hotel. All he could think about the entire way home was Ingrid Tulean. Ingrid Tulean, Ingrid Tulean, over and over again he said the name silently to himself, while picturing her beautiful face.

That night Benjamin lay in bed, eyes closed, trying to choose his dream from the millions of color dots he saw when he closed his eyes.

Benjamin had a theory that each and every one of those little color dots you saw when you closed your eyes was like a teeny tiny television screen, and each one of those color dots held a dream. He chose, and promptly fell asleep and dreamed of Ingrid Tulean. She was younger in the dream, his age, and oh how he loved her, oh how he didn't want the dream to end, oh how he never wanted to wake up. But, as life would have it, he did wake up, to his mother hovering over his bed, metal curlers in her hair and breath smelling of that horrid Listerine that she so loved to gargle with at every opportunity. That was some way to wake up, going from his young dream version of Ingrid Tulean, to the Listerine-smelling curlerhead looking down at him.

***

When they returned home to Los Angeles, Benjamin could not get Ingrid Tulean off his mind. He thought about her day and night. On his ninth birthday, his parents took him to a ritzy restaurant called Scampi, on La Cienega, and he thought about her while eating the very rich scampi. He even thought about her when he was throwing up the very rich scampi later that night. When his mother asked him what he wanted for Christmas, he wanted to say Ingrid Tulean, but instead he said something she would understand, this thing he'd seen at the store that would project a galaxy of stars on the ceiling.

It was odd that the Kritzers even celebrated Christmas, but Minnie and Ernie liked Christmas better than Hanukkah, apparently. Oh, they still lit the menorah, but Christmas was what the Kritzers loved, and they had a big tree with beautiful decorations, lights and tinsel and loads of presents waiting to be opened. Benjamin loved Christmas time and loved driving with his mother through Beverly Hills to see the beautiful homes all decorated and lit up, and the shops, and the Santas and sleighs strung across all the intersections. It was very magical, especially in the rain, and the Christmas of 1956 brought nothing *but* rain.

Christmas morning finally came and the brothers Kritzer, as usual, were first up and first to open their presents. As usual, they got some pretty great ones along with the usual dopey ones. Benjamin got his galaxy of stars machine, which he was very excited about. They had a visit from Esther and Louie Wish, Benjamin's favorites of his parents' friends. He loved Esther's flaming red hair and her good nature, and he loved Louie Wish because he would always do magic tricks and bring along his Polaroid Land Camera. Benjamin was quite enamored of that Polaroid Land Camera because it did its own form of magic trick; unlike any other camera, it took pictures and then you could see them instantly, instead of having to wait a week for them to come back from the developers. Louie and Esther stayed for dinner and Louie took a Polaroid Land Camera picture of the family Kritzer standing around the Christmas tree (with the menorah in the background).

That night, Benjamin plugged in his galaxy of stars machine. Suddenly, all over the ceiling were stars—it was just like being outside. There was a chart to help identify which stars and galaxies you were looking at and Benjamin studied that chart and stared at the stars and, of course, thought about Ingrid Tulean. Not even Jeffrey eating his bananas in bed could bother Benjamin—not when he had his stars and not when he was thinking of Ingrid Tulean.

***

New Year's Eve followed. Minnie and Ernie were going off to a party, and were, as Minnie put it, dressed to the nines. Benjamin asked why they were dressed to the nines rather than the eights or the sixes, but Minnie just ignored him and told him to mind Jeffrey, that Jeffrey was in charge. Benjamin would be allowed to stay up (if he could) until midnight if he minded Jeffrey. He told his mother that he minded Jeffrey a lot, but his mother said that wasn't what she meant.

That night, Benjamin did mind Jeffrey in the way that his mother meant, and, at the stroke of midnight (they knew it was the stroke of midnight because they called the Time Lady), the two of them screamed "Happy New Year" as loud as they could and toasted the New Year with a toasted marshmallow and a Coke.

Later, in bed, Benjamin looked at the stars on his ceiling, thought about Ingrid Tulean and wondered what 1957 would hold for him. Softly, he sang to himself

"Que será será,
Whatever will be will be
The future's not ours to see
Que será será
What will be will be…"

He closed his eyes, chose a dream from the thousands of color dots swimming before him and fell asleep.

Bruce Kimmel

PART TWO
1957

"They say for every boy and girl
There's just one love in this old world
And I know I've found mine."

—Tab Hunter, *Young Love*, Dot 45 15533

Bruce Kimmel

CHAPTER ONE
Susan Pomeroy

With Christmas vacation over, Benjamin returned to school to finish out the last few weeks of his B4 class. The good news was that he was going to have Mrs. Wallett again for A4 (the fourth grade was divided into halves, B and A) and his first half report card was not too horrible. The bad news was that Christmas vacation was over and summer vacation was a long way off.

The Bad Men were everywhere that January, dogging Benjamin's path at every turn. He took circuitous routes to school, ducked behind bushes to hide when he felt they were too close, and generally kept his mind and eyes alert in case they were to actually, for once, show themselves.

On weekend mornings he'd saunter over to Leo's Delicatessen, where he and Leo would discuss the events of the day over pickles and soda pop. Sometimes he'd go to the Saturday matinee or sometimes he'd go with Ernie down to The Erro. Sometimes he'd go to the park to watch Jeffrey play little league baseball, but Benjamin would soon become bored with the game and he'd wander around Rancho Park daydreaming, pretending he was Robert Mitchum trying to find Ingrid Tulean, while humming the music to *Foreign Intrigue*.

The Monday night dinners continued as usual. At one of them, after a particularly excellent Benjamin Kritzer Hour (he'd performed the Day-O song splendidly, dressed in his brand new calypso pants—after hearing the song, Grandpa Gelfinbaum remarked, "What is it, fish?"), his grandfather had barked at Benjamin to help his grandmother out of the chair and to walk her to the car. Benjamin looked at his 300-pound grandmother and said, rather incredulously, "Help my grandmother out of the chair? I can't help my grandmother out of the chair."

Minnie looked at Benjamin, all daggers, and said, "Don't be fresh, Benjamin. Do what Grandpa says."

"I'm sorry, my Charles Atlas course hasn't arrived yet. I'm still a ninety-eight-pound weakling in a sixty-pound body."

"Benjamin, you are not funny. Do you think you're funny? You help your grandmother out of that chair this minute and then you help her to the car or there will be no tomorrow for you."

Benjamin looked at the other people in the room.

"Can't three or four of you help me?"

"What are you, Danny Thomas? Help your grandmother up now!" Minnie said curtly.

Benjamin rolled his eyes heavenward and walked over to his grandmother. Jeffrey was sitting on the couch smirking and scratching his dinkle through his pants (his new favorite pastime). Benjamin looked at the huge mass known as his grandmother and said, "C'mon, Grandma, I'll help you up."

"Such a good boy."

Benjamin took hold of her hand and tugged and pulled with all his strength. He tugged and pulled and pulled and tugged, but the mass would not budge. He tugged and pulled some more and finally, miraculously, she came up off the chair. As she did, she exhaled a long "Oyyyyyyyyyyyyyyy," and pinched Benjamin's cheek, which was beet red from the exertion of the tugging and pulling. Benjamin held on to her hand as he walked her toward the front door, where everyone said their goodnights. Ernie had gone ahead to start up the Olds, and Minnie and Grandpa Gelfinbaum were just ahead of Benjamin and Grandma Gelfinbaum. Outside on the front porch, there was one step that led to the little walkway that led to the driveway where the Olds awaited. Benjamin went down the step, still holding Grandma Gelfinbaum's hand, but as she came down the step she lost her footing and even though Benjamin did his best to hold on to her, she fell to the ground emitting a horrible scream as she hit the pavement with a disgusting thud. Her scream caused Minnie to wheel around and scream, which caused Grandpa Gelfinbaum to wheel around and scream, "Oh, mein Got." His face was crimson and he had actually taken a bite out of his cigar and there were cigar bits mixed with spittle on his chin. He turned to Benjamin and pointed a quivering finger at him.

"Look vat you did! You kilt her. You kilt my vife!"

Ernie came running from the car and he and Minnie helped Grandma Gelfinbaum (who, other than having the breath knocked out of her, seemed to be fine) to her feet, while Benjamin helplessly looked on.

"You kilt her! Look at her, she'd dead!"

"I'm not dead. Do I look dead?" said Grandma Gelfinbaum, dusting off her black dress. "I fell. I'm fine. I have a little pain in my knee, that's all."

Grandpa Gelfinbaum stood where he was, shaking with rage, still pointing his finger at Benjamin, still holding his half-eaten cigar. "She has a pain in her knee! Look vat you did to my vife!"

Benjamin yelled at the top of his lungs, "I didn't do anything to your vife!"

Grandpa Gelfinbaum started yelling at the top of *his* lungs, "Whose fault was it then? *Amos 'n Andy*?"

Then Minnie chimed in, yelling at the top of *her* lungs, "Benjamin, don't make things worse. Go watch *I Love Lucy*."

Finally everyone calmed down and it was ascertained that Grandma Gelfinbaum was indeed fine. She wasn't dead, and aside from the pain in her knee, amazingly she hadn't been hurt at all. Minnie and Ernie loaded the Gelfinbaums into the Olds and Ernie drove them home. From that moment on, Grandpa Gelfinbaum rarely spoke to Benjamin, and, truth be told, that was perfectly fine with Benjamin.

Later that night, Benjamin was lying in bed, eyes closed, trying to choose a dream from the color dots, having no success. He opened his eyes and there was Jeffrey, looking down on him and saying, "You kilt my vife." Benjamin grabbed the fake vomit from the table next to him and threw it on Jeffrey, who threw it back at Benjamin who threw it back at Jeffrey who, by this time, was running around the room saying, "You kilt my vife, you kilt my vife" over and over again, with Benjamin chasing him now, until the voice of Minnie Kritzer thundered loudly from the den, "Shut up in there before you rue the day!" Jeffrey ran back to his bed and Benjamin ran back to his, and they both got under the covers. After a moment, Benjamin whispered, "You're going to rue the day. Rue. You're going to rue the day." Jeffrey giggled in his bed. Five minutes later, Benjamin whispered, "Rue." Five minutes later, Jeffrey whispered, "You kilt my vife." The "rue" and "vife" routine went on until one in the morning, when the brothers Kritzer finally dozed off to sleep.

***

February came and with it came Valentine's Day. Benjamin gave out lots of Valentine's Day cards and lots of candy hearts, and he got lots of cards and candy hearts in return but, since he didn't really have a special valentine, he wondered what the point was.

***

Benjamin was now in the second half of the fourth grade, and he continued doing well in spelling, reading and writing, and he continued doing horribly in arithmetic, geography and history. During those subjects he'd stare out the window, daydreaming, humming his new favorite song *Young Love* by Tab Hunter. He'd daydream being chased by the Bad Men, and he'd daydream his daring narrow escapes from them (once he was so immersed in his daydream that when he bolted back to reality he realized he'd been talking to himself out loud and pretending to hit one of the Bad Men—the rest of the class was staring at him as if he were a raving lunatic).

***

A week later Benjamin was on the lunch court, sitting on a bench eating his lunch (heinous bologna sandwich—why did his mother give him bologna sandwiches when she knew he hated bologna whether it was in a sandwich or not). It was one of those amazing Los Angeles days, with a blazingly blue sky and not a cloud in sight. He was glancing around the schoolyard when he spied a beautiful blonde girl sitting by herself on a nearby bench. And to Benjamin's utter amazement, sitting on that nearby bench was the spitting image of a nine-year-old Ingrid Tulean—the spitting image of the girl who had been in his dream that night in La Jolla several months back. He couldn't believe it, and he sat there, a piece of bologna foolishly hanging from his mouth like a second tongue, gaping at this thing of incomprehensible beauty. He finally came to his senses, wiped the piece of bologna away, wrapped up the remainder of his disgusting lunch and got up and threw it in the trashcan.

Trying to look as nonchalant as he possibly could (not very), he sidled his way closer to the nearby bench where the nearby young Ingrid Tulean was sitting. She was drinking from a straw, which was in a carton of milk, and she had her notebook open. Benjamin moved a little closer, then a little closer. He then took some coins out of his pocket and dropped them on the ground. The sound of dropping coins did the trick and Ingrid looked up from her notebook. She saw Benjamin kneeling down, picking up the coins and putting them back in his pockets. He looked at her and smiled his best Benjamin Kritzer smile. She smiled back and Benjamin could see the headlines in the *Herald Express*: NINE-YEAR-OLD DIES OF HEART ATTACK BECAUSE OF YOUNG INGRID TULEAN LOOK-ALIKE'S UNBELIEVABLY SPECTACULAR SMILE. He wanted so to speak, but it seemed he'd inadvertently thrown his voice away along with his bologna sandwich—nothing would come out. Finally, his voice was nice enough to come back, and he said, "Hi. I'm Benjamin. Benjamin Kritzer. 4th grade. Mrs. Wallett's class." He listened to those words coming out of his very own mouth and he wanted to brain himself and he would have if only his brain hadn't gone missing.

Young Ingrid Tulean looked at Benjamin, then replied, "Hi, Benjamin Kritzer, 4th grade, Mrs. Wallett's class. I'm Susan Pomeroy, 4th grade, Mrs. Bledsoe's class." And again, that dazzling smile. And again Benjamin died of a heart attack.

"I haven't seen you here before," Benjamin said.

"I haven't seen *you* here before, but then we only just moved here three weeks ago. We move a lot. That's what we do, we move. My father keeps getting relocated. This is my third school in the last year."

Before Benjamin could reply, the school bell rang and Ingrid-now-Susan got up and began to walk towards the trashcan to deposit her milk carton.

"Let me do that," said Benjamin, and he took the milk carton from her hand and bounded over to the trashcan where he deposited it with a great flourish. Susan laughed and that laugh made Benjamin's head go all fuzzy. The top of his mouth tingled in a way that it never did except when he ate Necco wafers. He ran back to her and walked alongside her as she started on her way back to Mrs. Bledsoe's classroom.

"Well, Benjamin Kritzer, 4th grade, Mrs. Wallett's class, you're going the wrong way."

"I know, I know… Listen, where do you live? You don't have to give me the exact address, just the area."

Susan looked at him and laughed again. "About three blocks from here, on Airdrome."

"I live off Airdrome! Can I walk you home after school? I mean, we go the same exact way."

"Well, I don't see why not, Benjamin Kritzer, 4th grade, Mrs. Wallett's class. You're the first person who's really been nice to me. Actually, you're the first person who's really talked to me. So, yes, I'd like it if you walked me home after school. I'll meet you at the gate, okay?"

And with that she flashed him that smile (heart attack number three) and went off into Mrs. Bledsoe's classroom. Benjamin ran all the way to Mrs. Wallett's classroom on the other side of the schoolyard—well, flew all the way, and he wasn't even wearing his Commando Cody Rocket Jacket.

***

As soon as the three o'clock bell rang, Benjamin was out the door of Mrs. Wallett's classroom faster than a speeding bullet. He sprinted to the gate with more power than a locomotive. In fact, if there'd been a tall building he would have been able to leap it in a single bound because he was SuperBenjamin and he was about to walk home the prettiest girl he'd ever seen. When he arrived at the gate, Susan was already there, leaning up against the fence in her pretty pink dress, matching pink shoes and pink cotton socks. Her blonde hair was in a ponytail tied with a pink ribbon—with all that pink she looked as soft and delicious as a big bunch of cotton candy.

On the way home they stopped at Marty's Bike and Candy Shop and Benjamin bought them some red licorice, which they ate while they walked down La Cienega towards Airdrome. Benjamin's heart was thud-thudding in his chest but it was a different kind of thud-thudding than when the Bad Men were rifling through the china cabinet in the middle of the night. This thud-thudding was new for Benjamin and he presumed it was because he was walking next to the most beautiful girl in the world and they were talking and laughing and eating red licorice.

While they walked and ate she told him the story of her life. How she and her father had had to relocate over and over again (her father worked for a textile company that had plants all over the country), how her mother had left her father when she was five (her mother had fallen in love with someone else and one day she simply wasn't there anymore), and how she didn't like to make friends because she was never sure how long she'd be living wherever she was living.

When they turned west on Airdrome, Susan led Benjamin down an alleyway that led to the back of the two-story duplex where she and her father lived.

"I'm up here," she said, pointing to the top of the stairs. "Well, thank you, Benjamin Kritzer, for walking me home."

"Thank you, Susan Pomeroy, for letting me walk you home."

"And thank you for the licorice."

"You're welcome for the licorice."

"Well, I'll see you tomorrow then."

She reached out and gave Benjamin's arm a squeeze and went up the stairs, opened the back door, tossed Benjamin a smile (heart attack number four and counting), and went inside.

Benjamin headed directly to Index Radio and Records where he bought the 45 of *Young Love* by Tab Hunter. As he walked home from there, Benjamin tried to memorize the feeling he'd had when Susan squeezed his arm. It was certainly the best arm squeezing feeling he'd ever experienced, that much he knew. When he got home, Minnie looked at him and remarked, "What happened to you? You look like you're on cloud nine."

"Is that good?"

"Is what good?"

"Cloud nine? Is there a cloud ten?"

"Nope, cloud nine is the best cloud."

"Then I'm on cloud nine."

Minnie looked at Benjamin and then felt his forehead to see if he had a temperature. His forehead felt just fine and dandy, thank you very much, and Minnie just shook her head and went into the kitchen.

And with that Benjamin floated into his room, elated to be on cloud nine rather than clouds one through eight. No, no other cloud number but nine would do.

***

Benjamin was in the middle of watching *Sheriff of Cochise* when the phone rang. He heard his mother, who was in the kitchen, answer it. The Sheriff of Cochise was driving around in his station wagon which had a rifle attached to the door, hunting down some Bad Men of his own. A moment later, Minnie was standing at the door to the den with a somewhat quizzical look on her face.

"It's for you."

Benjamin turned to her. "What's for me?"

"The telephone. It's for you."

"It's for me?"

"Do you see another 'you' around here? It's for you."

Benjamin walked down the hallway to the kitchen, followed closely by his mother. He couldn't remember a time when there'd been a phone call specifically for him. He went to the counter and picked up the receiver.

"Hello?"

"Hi, it's Susan. Susan Pomeroy."

As soon as Benjamin heard her voice he practically dropped the phone on the floor.

"Hi, hold on one second." Benjamin wheeled around to his mother and cupped the phone. "Do you have to stand there?"

"Well, excuse me for living," Minnie said and she walked out of the kitchen. Benjamin could hear her as she went down the hallway and informed Ernie that it was a girl calling. "A girl," Ernie said, "why would a girl call Benjamin?"

Benjamin uncupped the phone. "Sorry, I have very annoying Martian parents."

"I hope you don't mind that I called," Susan said, and her voice was so sweet Benjamin could hardly stand it. "I got your number from the phone book. Kritzer. Sherbourne Drive. Texas 0-2518."

Suddenly, Jeffrey zoomed into the kitchen. "A girl," he said, loudly and obnoxiously. He then burped one of his incredibly loud Jeffrey Kritzer champion burps. Very sweetly, Benjamin said, "Hold on one more sec, okay?" He then cupped the phone, turned to his brother and said, "If you don't get out I will tell our parents that you've been smoking. I will tell them that you have two *Playboys* hidden under your mattress. I will also stab you to death." Jeffrey gave Benjamin the finger.

Benjamin continued, "I will also tell that you just gave me the finger." Jeffrey burped again, even louder, and left the kitchen. Benjamin uncupped the phone.

"Sorry again. I also have an insane brother."

Susan laughed, and then said, "I just wanted to say thank you again for walking me home. I had a really good time."

"Me, too."

"Anyway, I'm just calling to ask if you'd walk me home again tomorrow."

Benjamin, amazed that she'd be asking such a question, answered as quickly as possible, "Are you kidding? Of course I would. I was going to find you tomorrow and ask you the same thing. Meet you at the gate?"

"Yes, meet you at the gate. Goodnight, Benjamin. Sleep tight."

She hung up before he even had a chance to say goodbye. He was suddenly sure that there had to be a cloud ten because cloud nine was just not going to cut the mustard anymore. He stared at the receiver, as if staring at it would somehow keep her there with him. He finally hung the phone up and turned around to go back to the den. Standing there in the hallway were Ernie, Minnie and Jeffrey, all looking at him. Minnie spoke first.

"What was that about?"

Jeffrey was next. "Yeah, what was that about?"

Ernie was next. "Why is a girl calling you?"

Benjamin glared at his father. "What am I, the measles? A girl can't call me?"

Minnie said, "You're only nine, Benjamin."

"Nine-year-olds can't get calls? Jeffrey got calls when he was nine. Jay Glotzer used to call him every ten minutes."

Ernie chimed in, "Jay Glotzer is a boy. Girls never called Jeffrey when he was nine."

"Why would they? Look at him. He burps, he farts, he picks his nose and wipes his boogers on the closet door. What girl would call him?"

In answer, Jeffrey burped loudly.

"Jeffrey, shut up," Minnie said.

"Yeah, Jeffrey, shut up," Benjamin said.

"You shut up, gonad," Jeffrey said.

Ernie's tongue began to dangerously protrude from his mouth, which meant there could be a licking in store for the brothers Kritzer if they didn't watch out. "Both of you, shut up and go to your room before I lose my temper."

The brothers Kritzer beat it to their room and shut the door. Benjamin was grateful, in fact, because he didn't want his Martian parents to continue asking annoying questions. Jeffrey left to go to the bathroom (Benjamin noticed that he'd snuck the *Playboy* out from under the mattress and put it under his shirt—when he snuck the *Playboy* out like that, Benjamin knew Jeffrey would be in there a long time—doing what he had no idea, nor did he care). Benjamin went in the closet, undressed, put on his pajamas and got in bed. He turned on the record player, put *Young Love* on the spindle and let it repeat over and over again.

Bruce Kimmel

They say for every boy and girl,
There's just one love in this old world
And I know I've found mine

He closed his eyes and Susan seemed to be in every color dot he saw.

The heavenly touch of your embrace
Tells me no one can take your place
Ever in my heart

Benjamin knew that he'd have none of his usual trouble getting up the next morning, knew that he'd leap out of bed, knew that he couldn't wait to get to school, knew that three o'clock couldn't come soon enough.

Young love
First love
Filled with true devotion

He imagined Susan squeezing his arm, flashing that smile, heard the sweetness of her voice on the phone.

Young love
Our love
We share with deep emotion

He was still thinking about her half an hour later when Jeffrey came back in the room. Jeffrey went to his bed, stashed the *Playboy* under the mattress and shut off the light. A moment later, Benjamin heard the hideous sounds of Jeffrey eating a banana and for once he couldn't have cared less.

CHAPTER TWO

Benjamin and Susan, The Story of Easter, and Passover

The next day at three o'clock sharp, Benjamin met Susan at the gate and walked her home (after stopping at Marty's Bike and Candy Shop for red licorice). From that day on, Benjamin walked Susan home from school every day (always stopping at Marty's for their daily dose of red licorice), and they would talk and laugh and share secrets and soon they were sharing lunches and recesses together, too. Benjamin was, to put it quite simply, smitten with Susan Pomeroy and Susan Pomeroy was, to put it quite simply, smitten with Benjamin.

***

Since Benjamin hadn't known Susan on Valentine's Day, when April first rolled around he gave her an April Fools' Day card, personally made by his very own self. It read HAPPY APRIL FOOLS' DAY BECAUSE I LOVE FOOLING AROUND WITH YOU OH AND BY THE WAY WOULD YOU LIKE TO GO TO THE MOVIES WITH ME ON SATURDAY? From your best fool, Benjamin Kritzer. He also gave her the 45 of *Young Love* because after all it was April Fools' Day and it seemed like an appropriately foolish thing to give her. Susan was delighted with her gifts and gave Benjamin a hug. Benjamin loved that hug, it was even better than the arm squeeze she'd given him several weeks earlier.

That weekend, on Saturday, they went to the Lido, where they saw a dandy double bill of *Attack of the Crab Monsters* and *Not of This Earth*. During intermission, Benjamin took Susan upstairs and showed her where the projection booth was, and told her the story of how he'd gotten to go in there and, unlike Jeffrey, she believed him. He also showed her his incredible rolling-down-the-stairs skill and she was properly amazed by the dexterity with which he negotiated the stairs as he rolled down them, lickety-split, one by one. He bought her a frozen U-No Bar, which she liked very much, and they shared buttered popcorn and a large coke. Afterwards, he walked her home and did a quite good impression of the crab monster.

Soon they were going to the movies every Saturday, sometimes to the Stadium (Benjamin's favorite local theater because of their giant Cinemascope screen), to the Lido, to the Picfair; whatever was playing, they saw it. They saw *The Spirit of St. Louis*, they saw a double bill of *The King and I* and *Bundle of Joy*, they saw *The Rainmaker* and *Written on the Wind*, and being with Susan at the movies made the movies even more magical than before.

Before heading off to the movie, they'd always stop at Leo's for a soda pop and a pickle (Leo adored Susan at first sight, yet another reason Leo was aces in Benjamin's book); then, after the movie, they'd invariably walk to the corner of Robertson and Pico and have hot dogs and Orange Juliuses. Susan loved Orange Juliuses; therefore, Benjamin loved Orange Juliuses. Of course, he'd had Orange Juliuses B.S. (Before Susan), but they never tasted as wonderful to him as they did A.S. (After Susan).

One Saturday, they were at the Stadium, seeing the very long movie *Giant*, with Rock Hudson and James Dean. They were sitting in the tenth row on the aisle (naturally), when Susan leaned over and whispered in Benjamin's ear.

"Want to feel the best feeling in the whole world?"

Benjamin, of course, thought that just being with Susan was the best feeling in the whole world and he didn't really see how there could be a better feeling in the whole world, but he whispered back, "Sure." She took his arm and began to lightly scratch the inside of it, up and down, from mid-arm down to the wrist and back again. Quite suddenly, Benjamin's brain turned to jelly, Benjamin's mind went fuzzy, Benjamin actually almost started to drool, and yes indeed, he had to admit, it really was the best feeling in the whole world. In fact, he would be content to just sit there for the rest of his life having Susan Pomeroy scratch the inside of his arm.

Lying in bed that night, he tried scratching the inside of his arm himself but it felt nothing like when Susan had done it. No brain jelly, no mind fuzz, no drool—no, Susan was simply going to have to scratch his arm forever, because Benjamin was now hooked on arm scratching.

***

When he wasn't with Susan he felt empty, empty the way his stomach felt when he was really longing for a Kentucky Boys hamburger. He thought, even then, that it was probably odd for a nine-year-old to feel that way but feel that way he did and there was nothing to be done about it. She'd given him her phone number (he'd already tried to look it up in the phone book but the number wasn't listed), which he'd memorized immediately (CR. 6-6326) and on weekend nights, when his mother and father were out playing cards or at a nightclub, and Jeffrey was busy with his friends, he'd call her and they'd talk for hours and hours. One time he'd asked her what she loved most and she answered without hesitation, hot fudge sundaes. How could you not like a girl who answered hot fudge sundaes? She loved his word fixation, and together they made up elaborate stories of why and how words were invented. Nostrils, for example. Benjamin just couldn't understand the kind of a mind that would come up with a word like nostrils. He and Susan imagined someone hundreds of years ago looking in the mirror and thinking, "Look at these holes in my nose. I know, I think I'll call them 'nostrils'." They'd written that one down in a notebook and laughed about it for days.

***

Easter was a few days away, and Mrs. Wallett had given her class an assignment—to write The Story of Easter. The Kritzers, like most people, celebrated Easter every year, even though they were Jewish. But, Benjamin didn't really have a clue as to what the real story of Easter was, other than it had something to do with Jesus Christ, hiding hard-boiled eggs, and rabbits (Susan, however, was not Jewish and knew all about Jesus Christ, so she filled him in as much as she could). He fretted for a day about the paper, but finally wrote his version of The Story of Easter, which he handed in to Mrs. Wallett.

Kritzer, Benjamin

Mrs. Wallett A4

April 16, 1957

THE STORY OF EASTER

Once upon a time in days of old there was a person named Jesus Christ. Jesus Christ said many wise things and people enjoyed Him very much. What Jesus enjoyed was boiling eggs. Oh, how He loved to boil eggs. After boiling a few, He would paint them with exciting colors. He loved those gaily-colored hard-boiled eggs. He hid them from His apostles, who would search for hours trying to find them—sort of like hide and seek, but with hard-boiled eggs instead of people. One April, He had boiled up a whole mess of eggs, painted them and hid them from His apostles. He thought, "I should make this an annual event, a holiday." As He was thinking it, He noticed that He was facing east. That gave Him the idea to call His new holiday, Easter. Just think, if He'd been facing west it would have been called Wester. Just as He named His holiday Easter, a bunny ran up to Him and wiggled its nose. Jesus Christ smiled at the bunny and thought to Himself, ah this must be the Easter bunny. And that is how the holiday of Easter came to be, and that is why we have Easter eggs and Easter bunnies. Many years later families all around the world still celebrate Easter and hide gaily-colored hard-boiled eggs, which the children must find. Even though my family is Jewish, we still have to find the gaily-colored hard-boiled eggs and we get little marshmallow bunny rabbits when we do. Sometimes Easter comes at the same time as Passover, and not only do we get to find gaily-colored Easter eggs, but we get to eat chopped liver, too. The End.

Benjamin got a B+ on his paper. On the top, Mrs. Wallett wrote: You are a very strange child, but I like you and I like your story of Easter. Please refer to your lessons regarding paragraphs. There are no paragraphs in your story and there should be paragraphs. Had there been paragraphs you would have received an A-.

Benjamin was thrilled with his B+, however, and he pinned The Story of Easter on the bulletin board in his room. When Easter arrived the following Sunday, he and Jeffrey searched for the hidden eggs (gaily-colored the night before by the family Kritzer sans Ernie, who was busy eating a meatloaf sandwich and watching Spade Cooley on channel five) and found all but one of them. The other egg went undiscovered because neither Minnie nor Ernie could remember where they'd hidden it. Every night for a week, Benjamin and Jeffrey hunted for the Undiscovered Egg (as it came to be known), but they never did find it.

Benjamin liked the fact that there was a gaily-colored hard-boiled egg lying somewhere, unfound. Oh, well, he thought, perhaps one of the Bad Men would find the Undiscovered Egg, when they got bored with rummaging around the china cabinet.

In the early Easter afternoon, he trotted over to Susan's house, but no one was home, so he left a package of yummy yellow marshmallow bunnies and a little white stuffed bunny outside her door, with a note that read: Happy Easter from Benjamin Bunny. The next day at school, she came running up to him at recess.

"Hello, Benjamin Bunny. I'll have you know I ate all my yellow marshmallow bunnies and I slept with my new stuffed bunny. I named him Benjamin after you-know-who."

She then gave Benjamin a big thank-you hug and handed him a shiny gold-wrapped chocolate Easter bunny. She smiled, and said, "To you from me. Don't sleep with it because it will melt and your sheets will look like a Three Musketeers bar."

Benjamin laughed, and then said, "Listen, next week is Passover."

"What's Passover?"

"It's a Jewish holiday. I was going to ask my Martian parents if you could come with us to temple and then eat with us. Do you think you could?"

"I don't know." She told Benjamin that she was worried that because she was Catholic that it might be a sin to go to a Jewish temple. Benjamin said he doubted it could be a sin since Jews celebrated Christmas and Easter and Jesus Christ seemed to be okay with that and so Benjamin was quite certain that it would be okay with Jesus Christ if

Susan went to temple and ate a Jewish dinner. That made sense to Susan, who replied, "Okay, I'll ask my father when I get home. That would really be fun. I'd get to meet your parents and your brother and your family."

"Well, yeah, there's that. Anyway, don't get too excited. I'm warning you now that they serve food with names like gefilte fish and chopped liver and matzoh and there's bitter herbs and this really awful stuff called charoses and they read a lot of Jewish words from a book for a really long time and all the men wear little beanies on their heads and we have to dip our pinkies in Manischewitz wine to cast out plagues."

"Sounds like fun."

"It isn't fun. Also, it smells really bad in my grandparents' apartment. But it'll be fun if you're there. We can give each other looks while we cast out the plagues and die from eating really hot horseradish."

The end of recess bell rang. Susan turned to head to her classroom, then looked back to Benjamin.

"Gefiltered fish? I'm not even going to ask."

Susan called him later that night to tell him that her father had said she could go. After he took his shower, Benjamin broached the subject with his mother.

"She's not Jewish is she?" Minnie asked.

"No, she's Catholic."

"Catholic? Feh. Why would a shiksa want to come to Passover?"

"She thinks it would be interesting. What's a shiksa?"

"Not a Jew. Benjamin, what is going on with this girl? You spend way too much time with her."

"She's my friend. I like her."

"It's not normal for a nine-year-old to be with a girl so much. So, what's going on with this girl?"

Benjamin just stared at his mother as if she were a can of Spam. She stared back and then said, "What's the matter, cat got your tongue?"

"Cat got my tongue? What does *that* mean?"

"It means does the cat have your tongue."

"Why would a cat have my tongue?"

"Exactly."

This was starting to feel like the *Abbott and Costello Show*.

"I don't want to talk about it," Benjamin said.

"Of course you don't want to talk about it. The cat has your tongue, how can you talk about it?"

At that moment, Ernie walked in, wearing only his pajama top, with his dinkle hanging there like the half-eaten salami on the porch, and said, "I thought I'd bring home some cracked crab for dinner tomorrow."

Minnie gestured toward Benjamin. "The cat has his tongue. He wants to bring that shiksa friend of his to Passover." She looked down at the hanging dinkle of Ernie Kritzer. "And why don't you put on some underwear before I throw up?"

Benjamin left the room and went to his bedroom. Just before he closed the door he heard Minnie say, "Fine, bring the shiksa, maybe she'll convert."

Thankfully, Jeffrey was in the den watching roller derby (Benjamin could hear announcer Dick Lane screaming "Whoa, Nellie!"), so

Benjamin turned on the record player, put on *Young Love* and thought about his blonde shiksa.

***

Susan arrived at the Kritzers precisely at ten o'clock on Passover morning (she was always very punctual). She rang the doorbell and waited. From inside the house she heard Benjamin yell, "I'll get it", followed by another voice (Jeffrey, she correctly presumed) yelling, "I'll get it", followed by Benjamin's voice yelling, "You answer that door and I will kill you with a kitchen knife", followed by a woman's voice saying, "Well, one of you idiots get the door", followed by Benjamin actually opening the door. "Hi, welcome to Mars." Susan smiled and came in the house. Directly opposite the front door was a closet with a full-length mirror on it. As Benjamin closed the door he turned around and saw Susan's and his reflection in the mirror. He thought they looked perfect together, he in his starched white short-sleeve shirt, black slacks (which he hated because they itched him), and oxfords, and she in her yellow striped dress and white satin shoes.

Jeffrey came down the hall, shirtsleeves fashionably rolled up and hair filled with Butch Wax, and Benjamin begrudgingly introduced him to Susan and waited for the worst. Surprisingly, though, Jeffrey was a perfect gentleman and merely said that it was nice to meet her and that he'd heard a lot about her from Benjamin. Benjamin took Susan on a tour of the brown living room, the swan dining room (where he pointed out the china cabinet that the Bad Men were so fond of rifling through), the kitchen (and the porch, where he showed her the much chewed hanging salami—which made her giggle madly), the den, with its ugly black and white linoleum, and finally his and Jeffrey's bedroom. By the time they headed back to the front of the house, Ernie and Minnie were there. Minnie was dressed elegantly in a tight fitting green dress and a hat that had a veil attached to it. Ernie was dressed in a black suit with a dark blue striped tie. Minnie looked at Susan for a moment, and then said, "You must be Susan."

Benjamin looked at his mother. "Who else would she be? Some girl who just happened to be passing by and stopped in to say hello?"

"Don't be fresh, Benjamin."

"Yes, I'm Susan. Susan Pomeroy. It's very nice to meet you, Mrs. Kritzer."

"It's very nice to meet *you*, Susan." Minnie gestured towards Ernie. "This is Benjamin's father."

"It's nice to meet you too, Mr. Kritzer."

"Very nice to meet you, Susan."

Benjamin's mouth was open so wide it was practically on the floor. Who were these people? Certainly they couldn't be his parents and his brother. They were being far too nice, far too cordial. He'd told Susan all about his Martian family and how positively weird they were and here they were being positively normal. Wasn't that just like parents who'd been Martianized? Pull the wool over everyone's eyes, that was their trick. Seem normal, then their son would seem like the insane one. This was their insidious plot, Benjamin was sure of it, and frankly this whole thing could have been a movie: Invasion of The Parent Snatchers. His thoughts were interrupted suddenly by the sound of his mother's voice.

"Close your mouth, Benjamin, you'll catch flies."

Ernie Kritzer opened the front door, and said, "Well, let's go. You know how Grandpa and Grandma are if we're not at temple an hour early."

They all exited the house and piled into the Oldsmobile, Jeffrey up front with Ernie and Minnie, Benjamin and Susan in the back seat. Ernie backed into the street, headed north to Pico and then turned left toward the beach. Susan surreptitiously moved her hand toward Benjamin and patted his hand as if to say, don't worry they're not fooling anyone. Benjamin smiled at her and she smiled back, and all was well with the world.

As they headed west on Pico, Jeffrey reached forward and turned on the radio and let forth with one of his ear-splitting burps. Minnie smacked him and said, "Jeffrey, for God's sake, must you? What will Susan think?" Susan was looking at Benjamin and giggling. Jeffrey, ignoring everyone, began to punch in different stations. This he did so fast that no one could even get an idea what song was being played on what station.

"Jeffrey, that's very annoying," Minnie said. "Leave it on one station."

Jeffrey punched another button and the voice of Pat Boone was singing

Oh, Bernadine,
You're the prettiest girl that I have ever seen…

Jeffrey's hand moved to change the station.

"Leave it," said Benjamin. "I love this song."

"You would, you booger," replied Jeffrey with a snicker.

"Let him hear the song," Minnie said. "And don't call your brother a booger. People in glass houses shouldn't throw stones."

Benjamin gave Susan a knowing look and Susan returned it with a knowing nod. The Oldsmobile zoomed down Pico with Pat Boone singing about the wonders of *Bernadine*, while Benjamin tried to figure out why people in glass houses shouldn't throw stones.

***

Ernie turned left on Main, drove down to Kinney, turned right and luckily found a parking space right away. The sky was a dark and dreary gray and there was a persistent wind blowing. They all walked over to the St. Regis Hotel where Grandma and Grandpa Gelfinbaum were waiting outside. Grandma was, as usual, dressed all in black, including a black hat and veil. Grandpa was dressed in a gray suit and was smoking his usual huge cigar. Everyone exchanged hugs and kisses, then Grandma Gelfinbaum waddled over to Susan.

"Is this the shiksa?"

Benjamin rolled his eyes heavenward. Minnie came over and said, "Mom, this is Benjamin's friend, Susan."

Susan smiled her sweetest smile. "Hi."

Grandma Gelfinbaum reached over and pinched Susan's cheek. "Oy, what a shayna punem, even if she isn't a Jew." She turned to Grandpa Gelfinbaum. "Gus, say hello, you rude shvantz."

Grandpa Gelfinbaum removed the cigar from his mouth, spit a huge glob of brown spit on the ground and said, "Hello. Let's go already, we dasn't be late."

They all headed south on the boardwalk, towards Rose Ave. Susan breathed in the smell of the salt air, which she really liked. It was the first time she'd ever been to the beach. She and Benjamin lagged behind the others, and Benjamin pointed out the sights to her as they walked along. They'd already boarded up the Pinochle Parlor and there were trucks and construction equipment everywhere, getting ready to convert Ocean Park Pier into Pacific Ocean Park. They passed the Dome Theater, which was "closed until further notice", then the boarded up Rosemary Theater and the Aragon Ballroom. The breeze whipped madly around them and Susan's long blonde hair whipped madly with it. They walked east on Rose over to Main Street and then south to the temple.

Outside the temple there were hordes of Jews congregating, most of them elderly, many of the men bearded and solemn, greeting each other with cries of "Good yontif". The men all had yarmulkes on, along with tallises, and the women were all dressed severely and most of them had veils over their faces. Benjamin hated those veils. To him they looked like spider webs and it gave him the willies.

After a while, everyone began going in the temple. Minnie told Benjamin that he didn't have to come in, that he could stay outside with Susan. That was just fine with Benjamin and even finer with Susan, who still thought it might be a sin to go into a Jewish temple. As soon as everyone was inside, Benjamin took Susan a bit north of the main entrance where there was a door. He opened it and took her inside. They walked down the staircase, which led to the basement. Benjamin had discovered the basement two Passovers ago, when, bored, he'd wandered through the door and down the stairs. It was just a large room with some chairs, but it had a microphone and a speaker and Benjamin had immediately turned on the microphone and sung many of his favorite songs with his voice coming over the loudspeaker system. He'd returned to the basement on every Jewish holiday and always did The Benjamin Kritzer Show Live from Temple.

Benjamin sat Susan down on one of the chairs, turned on the microphone and spoke into it as if he were Bob Hope or Danny Thomas or Jack Benny.

"Hello, I'd like to welcome Miss Susan Pomeroy to the basement of the temple. How are you today, Susan?"

From her chair Susan said, "I'm doing very well, thank you so much for asking."

"We're down here killing time until the ceremony is over and boy are my arms tired. But seriously, folks, here's a good one. A guy is walking down the street and coming towards him is a man with a banana in his ear. He goes up to the man and he says, hey mister you got a banana in your ear. The man looks at him and says, what? The guy says, a little louder, hey, mister you got a banana in your ear! The man looks at him and says, a little louder, what? The guy looks at him and yells,

YOU GOT A BANANA IN YOUR EAR! The man looks at him and says, I can't hear you, I've got a banana in my ear."

Susan giggled her mad little giggle and applauded.

"Thank you, ladies and germs. It was so cold this morning I fell out of bed and broke my pajamas. But enough about me. I'd like to sing a little song about our cleaning lady, Lulu Salmon." Benjamin grabbed the microphone stand as if he were Jerry Lee Lewis and sang, "Bee bop a Lulu, Lulu Salmon, Bee bop a Lulu, she's a lulu…"

Benjamin then ran through the rest of his repertoire, doing his renditions of *When The Red, Red, Robin Comes Bob, Bob, Bobbin' Along*, *Que Será Será* and, of course, *Young Love*. Susan, his audience of one, had a wonderful time and especially loved the fact that their cleaning lady was named Lulu Salmon. After an hour, they went back up and waited for the family to meet them, after which they all walked back to the Hotel St. Regis.

***

The Seder was, as usual, to begin at five, so Benjamin asked if he could show Susan around the pier. Minnie said yes, as long as they were back by four-thirty. Benjamin and Susan went downstairs and walked down the boardwalk and onto the pier. Not everything was open during the day, but luckily the House of Mirrors was. The big fat lady atop the House of Mirrors was laughing maniacally away as they entered. The House of Mirrors had always made Benjamin uneasy; he had the feeling that if he wasn't very careful he might get stuck in there for the rest of his life. They began negotiating the maze of mirrors very slowly, Susan staying very close to him. Benjamin turned to the left and promptly bumped into the glass. Susan said, "This way I think," turned right and promptly bumped into another pane of glass. They tried going straight and that worked. As they walked slowly and carefully, Susan took Benjamin's hand. Well, he didn't care if he bumped into glass or mirrors or anything else, so lovely was it having her hand holding his.

It took them roughly fifteen minutes of wending their way through the mirror and glass, but finally they did it. They entered the room with all the funhouse mirrors—mirrors that made them look short and squat, tall and thin and totally distorted. The closer you got to the mirror the more distorted you got. Benjamin pointed at the distorted Benjamin and Susan in the tall and thin mirror.

"Benjamin and Susan before dinner," he said.

They then turned toward the short and squat mirror.

"Benjamin and Susan after dinner."

They moved closer, getting even more short and squat.

"Benjamin and Susan after dessert."

They laughed and laughed and then, hand in hand, exited the House of Mirrors and headed over to the Penny Arcade. They played Skeeball, got a fortune from the fortune lady ("You will find romance" it said, and Benjamin put it in his pocket and saved it), and took their picture in the four-pictures-for-a-quarter booth. They waited outside the booth for the pictures to develop and when they slid down the slot Susan grabbed them. In the first photo both of them were looking straight at the camera as if they'd been caught by surprise. In the second photo,

Benjamin was looking straight ahead and Susan was looking at Benjamin. In the third photo Susan was looking straight ahead and Benjamin was looking at Susan, and in the fourth photo they were looking at each other with Benjamin's nose scrunched up against Susan's nose. It was late by then, so they hurried back to the St. Regis and got there in the nick of time.

***

When Benjamin and Susan got back to the apartment, Lena and Chaz and their kids Denny and Dee Dee were there. Everyone sat down at a big table, which had been assembled in the room with the Murphy bed in the wall. Grandpa Gelfinbaum sat at the head of the table wearing his yarmulke (as were all the males) and his tallis. Everyone had a Haggadah in front of them so they could read along with the Passover service. Thankfully, Benjamin was seated next to Susan. She'd opened her Haggadah and was trying to figure out which was the right side up. Benjamin turned the book the correct way and told her it was like reading backwards. She looked at all the Hebrew writing, which Benjamin explained to her was the story of Passover, and all the prayers they'd be saying.

Grandpa Gelfinbaum began the ceremony. The thing about Grandpa Gelfinbaum and the Passover ceremony was that you couldn't understand a thing he said. He read the Hebrew so fast it was incomprehensible. Susan sat there attentively, but she had no clue what was going on. She gamely ate the bitter herb and gamely ate the charoses, although she couldn't help but scrunch up her nose at the taste, and she dipped along with everyone else as they cast out the plagues. Then, Grandpa Gelfinbaum began the four questions.

"Ma nishtanah haleila hazeh mi-kol haleilot," he croaked in a sing-songy voice.

Minnie looked over at Susan and translated. "Why is this night different from all other nights?"

"There's a shiksa at the table?" Grandpa Gelfinbaum chimed in.

Grandma Gelfinbaum looked at her husband of forty years. "Read from the book and keep your mouth shut."

"How can I read from the book if I keep my mouth shut?"

"Such a pain in the tuchus, this man."

Minnie looked at Benjamin and said, "Benjamin, why is this night different from all other nights?"

"Because on this night we eat only unleavened bread," Benjamin replied, reading from the Haggadah.

Ernie looked up from the Haggadah and said, "Good. Unleavened bread. Can we skip the other three questions and eat now?"

"I have to finish," said Grandpa Gelfinbaum impatiently.

Grandma Gelfinbaum turned and said, "Then finish already, you yutz. Such a production he makes."

Grandpa Gelfinbaum hurried through the rest of the ceremony and then the food was brought to the table on big plates. First, everyone got a piece of gefilte fish. As soon as Minnie served Grandpa Gelfinbaum his he said, "What is it, fish?" Benjamin had told Susan all about Grandpa Gelfinbaum and "What is it, fish?" so as soon as he said it, she kicked Benjamin's leg under the table and tried not to laugh. She looked at her lump of gefilte fish sitting in the middle of her plate. Lena put a big dollop of horseradish next to it, and said, "Try it, it's homemade—delicious. The horseradish is homemade, too, nice and hot."

Susan cut off a small piece of the fish and dipped it into the horseradish, and then with some trepidation, put it into her mouth. Benjamin saw that she'd put way too much horseradish on it but before he could say anything the fish was in her mouth. The minute she swallowed, the lethally hot horseradish kicked in and she began to cough and sputter, and her eyes teared up as she coughed and sputtered some more. She coughed and coughed and sputtered and sputtered and everyone at the table thought it was so cute that she was coughing and sputtering. Her face was as red as the horseradish and Minnie came over and clapped her on the back while Benjamin poured her some water, which she gulped down as fast as she could.

"Nice and hot," Minnie said, "just the way Grandma likes it."

Susan finally recovered and glanced over at Grandma Gelfinbaum who was eating half her gefilte fish in one huge bite with an enormous pile of horseradish on it. She gulped it down and she began to cough and sputter, just as Susan had. Ernie went over to her and clapped her on the back until the coughing and sputtering subsided and Grandma Gelfinbaum smiled (there were bits of the horseradish in her teeth); then she gulped down the other half of the fish. Lena and Chaz both gulped down their gefilte fish, and they both began to cough and sputter at the same time. Chaz clapped Lena on the back and Lena clapped Chaz on the back. Denny and Dee Dee were also coughing and sputtering and everyone was clapping everyone else on the back. Jeffrey cut his fish up into little bits and spread them around his plate to make it look like he'd eaten some of it. Benjamin, of course, knew better than to go anywhere near the horseradish and he ate his gefilte fish dry.

Susan was very brave throughout the meal and tried the chopped liver (iffy), the matzoh ball soup (delicious), a piece of the brisket (yummy) and some noodle kugel (also yummy). Of course, as each dish was placed on the table, Grandpa Gelfinbaum would say, "What is it, fish?" Every time he'd say it, Susan would kick Benjamin under the table and try not to laugh. Every time she'd try not to laugh, Benjamin would start laughing and then she'd start laughing and then she'd kick him under the table again. By the time the dessert arrived (regular and chocolate macaroons, apple strudel and a huge white cake), Susan was ready to explode. In fact, she was sure she resembled what she had looked like in the short and squat mirror in the House of Mirrors. After dinner, the men went into the other room and smoked cigars and played Hearts, while the women did the dishes. Denny and Dee Dee left right after dinner, and Jeffrey watched *Sheena* on channel seven. Grandpa Gelfinbaum soon disappeared into the bathroom and moments later the most awful grunting and groaning sounds came from behind the bathroom door. Benjamin looked at Susan and suggested they go downstairs before everyone was invited into the bathroom to see Grandpa Gelfinbaum's Seder stool.

Downstairs, Benjamin and Susan sat on a bench on the boardwalk in front of the St. Regis. The air was chilly and Susan huddled close to Benjamin. The pier was almost totally devoid of people—word had gotten out that the pier was closing and for the last few weeks it had been all but deserted. Still, some of the lights were still lit and the sound of the roller coaster hurtling up and down on its tracks was as loud as ever.

Benjamin breathed in the cool crisp ocean air and Susan did the same.

"Isn't that the best smell," Benjamin said.

"I love it. I've never been to the beach at night before."

"I hope today wasn't too crazy."

"It was fun. Your family is fun."

"Well, yeah, unless you live with them."

"Benjamin?"

"Yes?"

Susan looked at him for a moment and then, trying to sound like Grandpa Gelfinbaum, said, "What is it, fish?"

Ernie's voice called out from behind them.

"We're leaving. Come say goodbye to Grandma and Grandpa."

They walked back to the hotel and everyone hugged, kissed and said their goodbyes. On the way home, Susan fell asleep, and her head rested on Benjamin's shoulder. Benjamin directed his father to Susan's house and when they got there Benjamin gently woke Susan and walked her up the back stairs. She yawned and smiled and thanked him for her wonderful Jewish day. She knocked on the door as Benjamin walked down the steps and back to the car. He stood there until he saw the door open and Susan go in, safe and sound.

CHAPTER THREE
Cinco de Mayo, Windy City and
The End of Ocean Park Pier

In preparation for Crescent Heights Elementary School's Cinco de Mayo celebration, Mrs. Wallett's fourth grade class went to Olvera Street. It was a lot better, Benjamin thought, than the last field trip to the tuna-canning factory. Olvera Street was filled with food stands and souvenir stands and had atmosphere to spare. They were told that this street had been the old trail that Governor Felipe de Neve led his colonists down when he founded the pueblo of Los Angeles in 1781.

The authentic music of Mexico played over loudspeakers and the smell of freshly made tortillas wafted through the air as Mrs. Wallett led the class down Olvera Street. They all got to eat authentic tacos along with authentic beans and rice, and they looked at piñatas and pottery and clothes and toured the entire street for nearly two hours before boarding the yellow school bus to return to school. On the way back, Barry Glazer farted mercilessly (as Ernie would put it, beans and Barry Glazer were not copasetic) and the bus reeked of his fetid fumes. The girls opened the windows which provided some relief, but every time it would get better, Barry would let forth with another noisy round, during which Barry would repeat and repeat, "It's not me, it's not me," as another burst would erupt from his rear end. When the bus pulled to the curb in front of the school, the class got out of that bus in record time.

***

Everyone in Mrs. Wallett's class had to get a white sheet from home and make their very own serape for the Cinco de Mayo celebration. The day before, the class spent three hours coloring their sheets with crayons and cutting a hole so they could slip them over their heads. Additionally, they all had to learn the *Mexican Hat Dance*. Benjamin could do many things but apparently doing the *Mexican Hat Dance* was not one of them. He couldn't learn the steps and the patterns and he kept bumping into people and turning right when everyone was turning left and turning left when everyone was turning right. Still, his serape was a work of art, with bold crayon colors making bold stripes up and down the sheet.

The next day, Cinco de Mayo, the whole school gathered on the playground and sat cross-legged on the pavement to watch the ceremonies. Benjamin loved when everyone sat cross-legged on the pavement because it afforded him wonderful views of the girls' underpants. It was a particularly windy Southern California day with the Santa Anas in fine fettle. The principal, Mrs. Peck, had hired authentic Mexican dancers to do the *Mexican Hat Dance* and to lead the ceremony. Mrs. Wallett's class was the one that had been designated to wear their homemade serapes and to do the dance after the professionals were through. Mrs. Peck introduced the *Mexican Hat Dance* people to everyone and everyone applauded politely. A Mexican sombrero was put on the ground and the *Mexican Hat Dance* music suddenly blared forth from a loudspeaker. The dancers took their places and began the dance. The señors wore beautiful serapes, with colorful shirts and pants, and large sombreros. The señoritas wore boldly colored skirts and scarves. They danced with tremendous skill and energy and looked like they were having the time of their lives, whooping and hollering with each and every step. At the end of the music everyone applauded loudly and the dancers responded with loud cries of "gracias".

Mrs. Peck then announced that it was time for Mrs. Wallett's class to do their version of the *Mexican Hat Dance* and to show off their homemade serapes. A hat was placed on the ground and the class stood and took their positions. Benjamin caught Susan's eye and just shook his head in dismay. She waved and smiled encouragingly at him. The real Mexicans began to clap as the music began. As the class started to do the first steps, the winds kicked into high gear and blew the Mexican Hat three feet across the pavement. The class immediately ran after it, trying to keep doing the steps as they did. As they reached it and danced around it, the wind blew the hat another five feet away. In the best of circumstances, Benjamin looked like a fool doing the *Mexican Hat Dance*. With the wind blowing the hat he was totally hopeless, forgot every step and finally ended up chasing the careening hat and sitting on the brim so the rest of the class could complete the dance. All the while, he whooped and hollered just as the real *Mexican Hat Dance* dancers had. The audience of kids and teachers laughed and applauded him for his clever solution to the problem (and the clever solution to not having to do his own inept dancing) and, as the music ended, he shouted "gracias" loudly. The real *Mexican Hat Dance* dancers shouted "gracias" in return and one of them picked up the sombrero and placed it on Benjamin's head. It was ridiculously large for him, but everyone laughed and applauded again (no one louder or more enthusiastically than Susan) and Benjamin ate up every minute of it.

***

The winds got worse over the next few days. In fact, they got so bad that branches of trees were strewn throughout the streets, and stray litter was gusting about like confetti. Trashcans were toppled as if they were cheap toys, and cars swerved and swayed involuntarily, not to mention dangerously.

That week, the Kritzers headed out to Ocean Park to visit Grandma and Grandpa Gelfinbaum and to pay a final visit to the pier, which was all but closed. The winds were terrible, buffeting the car like crazy and Ernie was having a hard time keeping within his lane of traffic. The radio was reporting that the winds were similar to the freak tornado that had occurred the year before in Alhambra; that weird event had ripped the tops off houses as if they were made of cardboard and caused much damage all around. Benjamin sat in the car listening while he looked out the window to see people trying to walk down the street but barely moving because the winds were so strongly against them. He wondered if this would turn into a tornado like the one in Alhambra (wherever that was), wondered if it would reach them and carry them all away like Dorothy in *The Wizard of Oz*.

As they turned right on Kinney, a lawn chair skittered across the street, blown from someone's backyard and now clickety-clacking its way to heaven knows where. As they all got out of the car they could barely hold on to the doors before the wind wrested them from their hands and slammed them shut. They walked down the street and turned right towards the St. Regis. Newspapers and debris were sailing through the air and sand was blowing along with it. The Kritzers shielded their eyes as they walked towards the hotel. Just as they reached the walkway, the wind surged even more strongly and literally lifted Benjamin off the ground. Minnie saw what was happening and screamed, "Oh, my God, grab him!"

Jeffrey, being nearest, reached out quickly and grabbed Benjamin by the back of his jacket and pulled him down.

"Hold him till we get inside," Minnie yelled, which she had to do to be heard above the howling of the wind.

Benjamin's heart was pounding, and he couldn't stop thinking of how he'd just been lifted right off the ground like that, by the force of the wind. It had almost been like flying, like Superman or Commando

Cody, but without a cape or Rocket Jacket. With Jeffrey holding on to him, they finally made their way inside the hotel lobby, where they quickly shut the door behind them. Minnie was shaking her head rather wildly back and forth.

"Benjamin could have blown away! I've never seen anything like it in all my born days." She turned to Benjamin. "Are you okay?"

"I'm okay," Benjamin answered.

"Jeffrey saved your life. Jeffrey, you saved his life," Minnie said.

Jeffrey got a maniacal grin on his face. "You owe me, booger. I saved your life. If it wasn't for me, you'd be halfway to Long Beach by now."

Ernie snapped, "Oh, don't make a federal case out of it. He got lifted off the ground a few inches."

"A few inches," Minnie said hysterically, "he was five feet off the ground for God's sake!"

"And I saved his life," Jeffrey said proudly. "He could have blown away."

Ernie looked at his oldest son. "Is it written somewhere that you have to be so annoying? Come on, lunch is probably on the table already. I'm starving."

"Food he thinks about. His child was five feet off the ground and he's thinking about lunch."

They all walked toward the elevator. As they got inside, Jeffrey whispered to Benjamin, "I saved your life. If it wasn't for me you'd be gone with the wind."

•

"I hate that movie," Benjamin said. Then he did a reasonable impression of Clark Gable. "Frankly, my dear, I don't give a damn."

"Benjamin said damn."

"Shut up, the whole kit and caboodle of you, before I brain you all," Minnie said, her teeth rattling around in her mouth like a bunch of Chiclets.

By the time they got upstairs and related the whole story to Grandma and Grandpa Gelfinbaum, Benjamin had been swept *ten* feet into the air and Jeffrey had had to leap and grab him to save him from certain death. Then they all ate canned salmon with onions and vinegar.

***

An hour later the wind had finally calmed down to a chilly breeze. Benjamin asked if he could go to the pier since it was officially closing that evening. Minnie said yes, but that Jeffrey had to accompany him, just in case any sudden winds erupted.

It was a sad sight, really, walking through Ocean Park. Benjamin's beloved Dome Theater was boarded up and many of the rides were shuttered. Grandpa Gelfinbaum's Wheel O' Fortune stand stood empty, looking lonely and abandoned. Still, on this final day, the rides that were open were free, and Benjamin and Jeffrey went on as many as they could, including the House of Mirrors, although the Fat Lady's laugh, even though it was the same as always, seemed hollow and mirthless. They also went on Toonerville and played Skeeball at the Penny Arcade. They rode the merry-go-round one last time, although there was no brass ring to reach for. Best (and worst) of all, they had their final Vanilla Custard Ice Cream cone (also free), and Benjamin thought that that is what he'd miss most of all.

As they walked back toward the boardwalk, Benjamin looked at the signs plastered onto the boards that now surrounded the Dome Theater. They promised the most wonderful amusement park in Southern California: Pacific Ocean Park, coming to Santa Monica in June of 1958. Wonderful amusement park though it might be, the pier would never be the same without the Vanilla Custard Ice Cream stand, the Dome Theater and yes, Grandpa Gelfinbaum's Wheel O' Fortune. Benjamin could still taste the vanilla custard ice cream as he and Jeffrey walked slowly back to the St. Regis. It was a taste he knew he'd never forget.

CHAPTER FOUR

Summer

By the beginning of June, the crazy May winds had died down and it looked like it was going to be a typical and glorious Los Angeles summer. School was coming to an end, and Benjamin looked forward to spending a good deal of his time with Susan.

Minnie was suffering from migraines, and corns on one foot and bunions on the other (corns and bunions sounded like a vegetable medley to Benjamin) and she did very little but complain endlessly. One minute it would be "my head is killing me," and the next it would be "my feet are killing me." Benjamin thought that was a funny way to put it, and he imagined what the headline in the *Herald Express* would look like: WOMAN KILLED BY OWN HEAD! In fact, he thought that was so funny that he drew a mock-up of a *Herald Express* newspaper, complete with all the front-page stories. Under the headline was the story, written by reporter Benjamin Kritzer:

> Today, a woman was killed by her own head. "It was shocking," said her neighbor, Lydia Frip. "Her head just up and killed her…just like that. I've never seen anything like it." Police said the woman's head had a long history of odd behavior. The Chief of Police said they were doing everything possible to bring the woman's head to justice.
>
> In a related story, another woman was killed by her own feet. Just prior to the event, she was heard to say, "My feet are killing me," but apparently no one believed her. The citizens of Los Angeles were warned to be on the lookout for the killer feet. Detective Joe Thursday said, "These feet are extremely dangerous. They've already killed one woman and there's no telling if they'll stop there. If you see any suspicious feet, please call the police immediately and do not engage the feet in conversation."

Benjamin showed his faux newspaper to his mother, who did not see the humor and said, "Benjamin, go play in traffic."

"Why do you always say that? What if I went out and played in traffic and got hit by a truck? How would you feel then?"

"Well, that would be a fine kettle of fish."

Benjamin looked at his mother as if she were a package of headcheese. "If I got hit by a truck it would be a fine kettle of fish?"

"Exactly. Benjamin, enough. I've told you and I've told you, they're just sayings. Now leave me alone. I have to soak my bunion."

That seemed like a good exit line and Benjamin left his mother's room. He walked through the den where the television was on; Ernie was in his chair snoring loudly as Dinah Shore was imploring everyone to see the U.S.A. in a Chevrolet. Benjamin left the den and passed the hall bathroom. The door was closed which meant Jeffrey was in there again. It seemed like nowadays he spent hours and hours in there, doing heaven knew what.

Benjamin wondered if all families were like this or if his was just uniquely odd.

***

The final day of school was a short one, ending at noon. Benjamin got his report card, which was surprisingly good. He went up to Mrs. Wallett and thanked her and she thanked him right back for brightening up both her class and her whole semester. She gave him a hug and wished him a happy and sunny summer.

He met Susan at the gate and they decided to go have cheeseburgers and malts at Fosters Freeze. Afterwards, they walked over to Ralph's Five and Dime and Benjamin bought a model kit of a 1956 Thunderbird. This was Benjamin's new thing; he would buy model kits but not follow the directions and just glue the parts on any way he saw fit to glue them. This made for some interesting-looking models, of that there was no doubt. For example, he'd done a beautiful job with a hot rod model kit. By the time he'd finished with it, it looked like some weirdly shaped rodent, and he displayed it proudly on his bedroom table (well, his half of the bedroom table).

Benjamin and Susan brought the model back to her house and they worked on that 1956 Thunderbird for the rest of the afternoon. It turned out to be a masterpiece, in Benjamin's humble opinion. The doors were on the hood and trunk of the car, the tires were sitting where the doors would normally be (normal didn't enter into this, however), the steering wheel adorned the front bumper, and the seats were hanging over the sides of the car. It was a true work of art and they named it Ralph.

It was an auspicious beginning to summer vacation and Benjamin somehow knew that this was going to be an extraordinary summer.

***

The Bad Men were still frequenting the Kritzer house but it seemed to Benjamin not as frequently as they used to. Oh, to be sure, he'd still wake up in the middle of the night and hear them rifling through the china cabinet or creeping down the hall, but he was not quite as frightened as he'd been in the past and he seemed to fall asleep again without breaking into a cold sweat. The Bad Men still followed him here and there but he had less time to be concerned with it because he and Susan were basically inseparable.

***

In addition to building the Benjaminesque model kits, Benjamin had also discovered something else he was crazed with, and that was spelling backwards. How it happened was this: He and Susan had their Word Notebook and it was becoming filled with their favorite words and their versions of how those words were created. Their latest entry was a doozy (in fact, truth be told, the word "doozy" was a "doozy" and could only have been made up by a person who was also a "doozy"). Phlegm. There was simply no explanation that one could come up with to explain the word phlegm. It just sat there like so much fish (as Grandpa Gelfinbaum would say), looking incredibly stupid. First off, what was the "ph" doing in the word when an "f" would have been far more appropriate? Then there was the little matter of the "g". Just what in heaven's name was that "g" in there for? You didn't pronounce it, and it didn't look aesthetically pleasing, so what was the point? It looked like someone had just taken a bunch of letters, thrown them in the air and let them land. But the real point was who came up with the word in the first place? Who decided that the disgusting mucous junk that you'd cough up during a cold should be called "phlegm"? Somewhere, someone had coughed up some yellowy guck, looked at it and said, "Ah, I think I'll call this yellowy guck 'phlegm'." "Phlegm", of course, naturally led them to the word "snot". And "snot" was how Benjamin discovered spelling backwards.

Jeffrey had gotten a summer cold and his nose was running like crazy. Used Kleenex was strewn all around the bedroom and Jeffrey just lay in bed, blowing his nose and blowing his nose and blowing his nose.

It was all quite disgusting. In any case, Benjamin was relating this to Susan one day and he said, "I can barely even walk in the bedroom, there's Kleenex all over the floor filled with snot." Susan giggled her mad giggle when she heard that word.

"Ooh, let's add 'snot' to the book," she said. "Not real snot, just the word."

"You add it. I can't add it; I've seen way too much snot in the last two days. I've seen tons of snot."

Susan opened the book and wrote "tons of snot" down. Benjamin looked at it and it was almost like a bell went off, like on one of those television quiz shows.

"Of course he has tons of snot," Benjamin said in an amazed voice.

"Huh?"

"Don't you see? Tons of snot. Tons spelled backwards is snot!"

Susan looked at what she'd written and couldn't believe it herself.

"Wow."

"Wow is right. Wait, 'wow' spelled backwards is 'wow'."

"Wow."

They were both giddy at the spelling backwards discovery and from that moment on spelling backwards was incorporated into their Word Notebook, and they added new entries every day. "Poop" spelled backwards was "poop", "mom" spelled backwards was "mom", same for pop, dad, did, boob, noon, tot and yay. But Benjamin liked words that became different words when spelled backwards: pan/nap, part/trap, live/evil, pot/top—well, the list was practically endless. But their favorite was when they spelled backwards and could make up whole new words, all their own, that could mean anything they wanted them to. They'd started that variation on spelling backwards by looking at the word "proof" one day and coming up with "foorp". "Foorp" became their word to describe people they didn't like. Practically everyone on Benjamin's block was a foorp. Paul Needle, the egg sucker, was the biggest foorp of all. Some of their other favorite made-up spelled backwards words were yobwoc, redwop, malc, and wollof. Of course, they began calling each other by their spelled backwards names—Nimajneb and Nasus, which made them sound like they were a Biblical comedy team.

Benjamin's finest spelling backwards hour came one afternoon when his mother was feeling particularly horrid (what else was new—her feet bothered her, her head bothered her, her false teeth bothered her) and was, as she put it, stressed beyond repair. The television quiz show bell rang in Benjamin's head and he said to his mother, "If you're so stressed you should eat desserts."

"Why? Desserts will make me feel less stressed?"

"Yes!"

"Why?"

"Because stressed is desserts spelled backwards." He waited for his mother's amazed and thrilled reaction. Of course what he got was, "Benjamin, you are an idiot. You're driving me crazy!"

That was not a very long drive, in Benjamin's opinion. That was just a short trip around the block, in Benjamin's opinion. And she could call him an idiot all she liked, but stressed/desserts was brilliant and he knew it. He called Susan and told her and she was suitably impressed and she immediately entered it into the Word Notebook.

CHAPTER FIVE
Hollywood

Ever since he'd first seen the Cinerama logo, Benjamin had wanted to see one of the movies made in that process. He didn't exactly know what that process was; he'd just heard that it was the biggest, most amazing movie screen ever—bigger than Cinemascope, bigger than Todd AO (his parents had just taken him to *Around the World in Eighty Days* at the Carthay Circle, and he couldn't imagine anything bigger than that), bigger than big. Checking out the ads in the *Herald Express* he saw the one for the new Cinerama movie, *Seven Wonders of the World*, which had just opened at the Warner Cinerama Theater on Hollywood Blvd. Benjamin loved Hollywood and hadn't been there since his parents had taken him to the Paramount to see Dean Martin and Jerry Lewis in

Pardners. So, he decided it was time for him to experience Cinerama, and he asked his father and mother if he and Susan could go see it.

"Isn't that reserved seats? Isn't that expensive, doesn't that cost two dollars?" Minnie asked.

Yes, Benjamin told her, it was expensive, yes it was reserved seating and yes, he wanted to see it and wanted to see it with Susan. Minnie looked at Ernie. "What do you think? I think he sees too much of that girl."

Ernie yawned noisily and said, "I think I'd like a bologna sandwich. I think if someone made me a bologna sandwich and brought me some ice water with it that they'd have an excellent chance of going to that movie, that's what I think."

Benjamin was in the kitchen in three seconds making the best bologna sandwich (lots of mayonnaise, which made Benjamin want to gag) on white bread and getting a nice tall glass of ice water from the ice water spigot attached to the refrigerator (Ernie was very proud of being the only one in the neighborhood to have such a thing on his refrigerator). Benjamin brought the sandwich and water into the den and gave it to his father. Ernie pulled ten dollars out of his pocket (he always carried a huge wad of cash with him) and handed it to Benjamin.

"Go, take your friend, have fun. But we're not driving you, you take the bus."

Benjamin thanked his father, then ran to the kitchen and called Susan to tell her they were going to Hollywood to see *Seven Wonders of the World* in Cinerama and that afterwards he had a big secret surprise planned for her. Since Susan loved big secret surprises, she was very excited and said she'd find out all the necessary information about which bus would get them there (Benjamin didn't know from buses).

"I'll be at your house at ten-thirty," Benjamin said.

"Okay. See you tomorrow, Nimajneb."

"See you tomorrow, Nasus."

Benjamin hung up and went into his room, where he drew some Cinerama movie screens and thought about the big secret surprise he had for Susan.

***

The next morning, Benjamin met Susan in the alley and they walked to La Cienega. Their bus pulled up a few minutes later; they boarded it and sat down in the back. As the bus traveled north on La Cienega, Benjamin pointed out some of his favorite places, like Dick Webster's (home of the Lemon Meringue pie), and a bit further north (on La Cienega's Restaurant Row) the Kritzers' favorite expensive restaurant, Lawry's Prime Rib, not to mention Stears For Steaks and Richlor's, Home of The Planked Steak (Benjamin loved the planked steak, especially the mashed potatoes which lined the wooden plank). The bus continued north and when they stopped at the red light at Beverly Blvd., Benjamin pointed out Kiddieland on the southwest corner. Kiddieland was a charming place located in what was called Beverly Park, and Benjamin had been there many times, riding the ponies and taking the train ride around the park. It was famous as the place where all the divorced movie stars took their kids, and indeed Benjamin had seen several actual movie stars with his own actual eyes.

When they reached Sunset Blvd. they had to transfer to another bus. The second bus took them east toward Hollywood. They got off at Wilcox and walked two blocks north to Hollywood Blvd. where the Warner Cinerama Theater was located. They bought their reserved seat tickets (excellent center seats the box office person said) for the two o'clock show. They had at least an hour-and-a-half to kill, so they walked over to Sunset and Vine so Susan could see the NBC Studios (Ernie had taken Benjamin and Jeffrey there to be in the audience for *Juke Box Jury* with Peter Potter) and that wonderful and magical place known as Wallich's Music City ("It's Music City, Sunset and Vine" sang the lady on the radio commercial). Wallich's Music City was the premier record store in Los Angeles. They had everything—any record you could possibly want, no matter how arcane, they had. They also had listening booths where you could preview the records.

They went into the store and spent an hour looking through bins and bins of both long-playing records and 45s. They took several 45s into the listening booth. Their favorite was a brand new single by Jimmie Rodgers called *Honeycomb*, on Roulette Records. They played that one several times and Benjamin ended up buying it.

They headed back to the theater, got there at one-thirty and presented their reserved seat tickets at the entrance. It was a beautiful theater; the lobby had intricately-patterned rugs, and the walls were adorned with inlaid gold figures and designs. Benjamin eyed the huge staircase, which led to the balcony, but decided this was too ritzy a place to go tumbling down the stairs.

They went to the candy counter and got some buttered popcorn and a drink to share. He also bought a souvenir program for him and Susan to share. They then showed their tickets to an usher who showed them to their very own reserved seats. Benjamin liked the fact that only they could sit in these two particular seats. For this showing of *Seven Wonders of the World*, these were the Benjamin and Susan seats and if someone else wanted to sit in them they were out of luck.

The first thing that Benjamin noticed as they were walking down the aisle were the three immense booths at the back of the theater: One on the left, one in the middle and one on the right. They all had those little portholes so he knew that those must be the projection booths. The second thing he noticed as they took their seats, was the largest set of drapes he'd ever seen in his life. They were sort of a maroon color and they practically engulfed the entire front of the theater.

According to the souvenir program, Cinerama was shown with three projectors running simultaneously. The drawings and diagrams in the program looked amazing to both Benjamin and Susan and they couldn't wait for the feature to begin. Benjamin liked reserved seat engagements; it seemed everything was much more hoity-toity, to coin one of Minnie's more amusing phrases. Everyone was dressed nicely and the whole thing had an air of expectancy, of something special about to happen, which, Benjamin supposed, was the point. They ate the popcorn and perused the souvenir program while people streamed into the theater, eventually filling all of the reserved seats. Finally, the lights dimmed. Those magnificent curtains began to part and Benjamin and Susan couldn't wait to see the huge splendor of that giant screen. Unfortunately, the curtains only parted a few feet and stopped. The screen that was revealed was tiny, even smaller than the Picfair. A black and white image came up on the tiny screen and someone named Lowell Thomas began to speak.

Benjamin looked at Susan with a "this is *it?*" look on his face. This was Cinerama? This was the big deal? The sound was tinny and the image seemed like a television screen in the cavernous theater. Benjamin couldn't even focus on what Lowell Thomas was prattling on about, so disappointed was he. But then, after about five minutes, Lowell Thomas walked closer to the camera and in his stentorian voice said, "And now, let's put on our seven league boots and go to the seventh wonder of the world." And with those words, Benjamin's movie-going world changed forever.

A cymbal crashed loudly and all of a sudden the curtains parted and other curtains went up and the huge curved Cinerama screen was revealed in all its glory, with the most stunningly beautiful images Benjamin had ever seen. Nothing had prepared him for the grandeur he was experiencing. It was almost like he was *in* the picture, almost like he was there, so clear and crisp and real was the image. And the sound. The sound came from everywhere. From behind the screen, from the sides of the theater, from behind them, from the balcony. There were scenes shot from an airplane, scenes shot from a train, and every time one of those scenes would come on, he and Susan and the rest of the audience would ooh and aah because it felt as if they were part of the action, that they were on the train or in the plane. It was, in a word, stupefying. After a while, Benjamin could see where the images overlapped each other from the three separate projectors, and he pointed that out to Susan.

After the film was over, he wanted to stay and see it again, but reserved seat movies were not like regular movies where you could sit in the theater all day if you liked and see the same show over and over again for the one admission price. No, Cinerama only had three showings a day and you had to pay each time. As he and Susan exited the theater he couldn't stop talking about how incredible what they'd seen was. It wasn't really a movie movie, he knew that, but still whatever it was it was one of the best things he'd ever seen.

***

The sun was blinding as they came out from the darkness of the theater. Hollywood Blvd. was bustling with people on this summer afternoon—people window-shopping, people going to restaurants, people just having a leisurely stroll. Susan took Benjamin's hand in hers and said, "So, when do I get my big secret surprise?"

"In a little while. We have to walk to where it is."

They headed west towards Highland. They walked hand in hand (they'd begun holding hands regularly ever since they'd done so in the House of Mirrors), and they noticed more than one person looking at them strangely, which bothered them not one or even two whits. They walked slowly, looking at all the stores. They spent quite a bit of time looking in the window of Bert Wheeler's House of Magic, checking out the Jerry Mahoney dummy, the horror movie masks, and the magician's wands and hats and capes and tricks.

They crossed Highland, spent a few minutes looking at the footprints at Grauman's Chinese and then continued on to the next block. Benjamin stopped at the corner.

"Okay," he said, "your big secret surprise is coming up."

"Tell me," she said. "What is it?"

They walked ahead a few more feet and stopped again.

"What do you love most?"

"You know. Hot fudge sundaes."

"Voila." He turned her toward the building they were standing in front of. She looked at the name on the window.

"C.C. Brown's? What's C.C. Brown's?"

"Only the best hot fudge sundae in the whole wide entire world."

Susan's eyes lit up like a hundred watt bulb. "The best hot fudge sundae in the whole wide entire world? Why are we standing out here?"

He ushered her inside where they were seated at an empty table. It was fairly empty in C.C. Brown's at this time of day. Most of their business came in the evening when people would stop in after seeing a movie on the boulevard. Menus were brought to their table, but Benjamin told the waitress that they didn't need them. He ordered each of them the one and only C.C. Brown's hot fudge sundae. While they waited for the sundaes to arrive, Benjamin told her that this was one of his mother's favorite places and, whenever they came to the movies in

Hollywood, they'd always stop at C.C. Brown's afterwards for a hot fudge sundae. It was a Kritzer tradition.

The sundaes arrived. To Susan they didn't look like any hot fudge sundae she'd ever seen. This was very compact, this hot fudge sundae was. In a silver cup sat one scoop of ice cream. On top of the ice cream was whipped cream and nuts. No cherry. And no hot fudge. Benjamin saw the confused look on her face and said, "As my mother would say, you can't judge a book by its cover."

He pointed to the little brown ceramic pitcher next to the silver cup and told her the hot fudge was in there and that she should pour it onto the sundae herself, but very carefully, because if you weren't careful all the hot fudge would pour out at once. She watched Benjamin expertly pour out some hot fudge onto his sundae, just the right amount to cover some of the whipped cream and ice cream. She did the same and she managed to do so almost as expertly as Benjamin. He watched expectantly as she took her first bite. As soon as her spoonful of sundae hit her mouth, the expression on her face became so blissful that it actually made Benjamin laugh out loud.

"What?" Susan asked through her mouthful of sundae.

"You should see your face. I take it that means you like it?"

"Benjamin, this is the best thing I ever ate."

"Told you."

And with that, Benjamin dove into his sundae, and the two of them sat there in hot fudge sundae heaven, alternately taking bites and pouring more hot fudge from the little brown ceramic pitcher. They both finished every single bit of their sundaes and sat there, totally sated.

Finally, Benjamin paid the check and they walked out onto Hollywood Blvd. They walked over to La Brea and then walked south to Sunset.

As they waited for their bus in front of the Carolina Pines Coffee Shop, Susan said, "They should change the name of that movie to Eight Wonders of the World because C.C. Brown's is definitely a Wonder. In fact, I'd make it the first Wonder of the World. Well, maybe second. You're the first Wonder of the World, Benjamin Kritzer."

Impulsively, she leaned over and kissed him on the cheek. Benjamin had thought it impossible that anything could top a C.C. Brown's hot fudge sundae or, for that matter, Susan's arm scratching, but she'd just proven him wrong. He never even heard the bus arrive.

CHAPTER SIX
The Transistor Radio,
and Stargazing

One day, Benjamin was leafing through a magazine at Daylight Market when he came upon an ad for a brand new Sony transistor pocket radio. He marveled at how small it looked in the picture—not like the big clunky stupid-looking radio he and Jeffrey had in their room. No, this radio fit in your actual shirt pocket (or so the ad said) and it operated on batteries and, best of all, it had an earphone so you could listen to it with no one else hearing. Well, he simply had to have it. There was no way he was not having it and that was that. *How* he was going to have it was another story.

He walked back home, thinking of the brand new Sony transistor pocket radio. Even the name was magical. Oh, yes, he was going to have to really turn on the Benjamin Kritzer charm in order to get his parents to buy him his very own Sony transistor pocket radio.

After dinner that night, Ernie retired to the den to watch television and Jeffrey retired to the bathroom to do whatever he did in there twelve times a day. Minnie was washing the dinner dishes. Benjamin walked up beside her and said, "Do you want me to dry?"

Minnie turned and looked at him and immediately felt his forehead to see if he had a fever. "You're offering to dry the dishes?" She cast a suspicious look at him. "Why? Did you do something wrong? Did you break something?"

"No, I didn't break anything. No, I didn't do something wrong. I just thought you might like to have me dry."

"Benjamin, I wasn't born yesterday. Are you in a pickle of some sort?"

"Am I in a pickle? How can a person be in a pickle? A pickle is a pickle, it's too small for a person and anyway why would anyone want to be in one?"

"You know what I mean, Mr. Smart Guy. In a jam, are you in some sort of jam?"

"Am I in some sort of jam? Yes, I'm in some grape jam. What does that *mean*? First I'm supposed to be in a pickle and then I'm supposed to be in a jam. What am I going to be in next, a hot dog?"

"Benjamin, don't be an idiot, you can't be in a hot dog. You know very well what I mean. Are you in trouble, did you do something?" As she continued, she began to raise her voice. "Why are you offering to dry the dishes when you've never offered to dry the dishes in the entire history of your entire life? Something is rotten in the State of Denmark."

"Is it a pickle?" This was not going at all well, not going at all the way he planned. He needed to stop being Mr. Smart Guy if he was going to get his brand new Sony transistor pocket radio. "I was just asking if you'd like help drying the dishes, after you worked so hard cooking dinner."

Minnie turned to Benjamin, not even noticing that her hands were wet and dripping water all over the floor. "All right, Benjamin, what do you want? You obviously want something and I want to know what it is you want because you are truly starting to give me a migraine and you're making me nauseous with all this sweetness and light."

Benjamin gathered his courage and blurted out, "Would you buy me a Sony transistor pocket radio? It could be an early birthday present." He smiled his best Benjamin smile.

Minnie frowned her best Minnie frown. "A what? You want me to buy you a what?"

Benjamin got the magazine and showed her the ad for the Sony transistor pocket radio. Minnie glanced at it.

"Why do you need this so bad? You have a radio."

"I know, but it's so big and ugly and this fits in your pocket and has an earphone and I won't have to blast the house with music and annoy you when you have a migraine."

That made a modicum of sense to Minnie. Not having the radio blasting music was a definite plus.

"And you would accept this as an early birthday present?" Minnie asked.

"Yes, yes, yes."

"And you wouldn't conveniently forget that you got an early birthday present and expect another one?"

Well, of course he would, but he kept that to himself. "No, no, no. I won't forget and I won't expect another present, I promise."

"And you promise no more blasting loud music?"

"I won't need to, I'll have my earphone."

Minnie tapped her foot for what seemed like an eternity, then said, "Okay, Benjamin, tomorrow we'll go to White Front and see if they have it."

Benjamin literally jumped up in the air with glee. "Thank you, thank you, thank you!"

"Why are you saying everything three times?"

"Happy, happy, happy."

"Don't push your luck, Mr. Smart Guy."

Benjamin, happy as a clam (which, of course, spelled backwards was one of his favorite Benjamin and Susan words, malc), turned and started to bound out of the kitchen.

"Hold on there a minute, Kemosabe."

Benjamin turned around and saw his mother holding the dishrag. "I believe there are some dishes you'd like to dry," Minnie said. Benjamin had no choice—he sauntered back to the sink and began drying, while visions of the Sony transistor pocket radio danced in his head.

***

The next morning, bright and early, Minnie and Benjamin drove downtown to the White Front store. Benjamin was so excited he could barely contain himself. Once inside, Minnie asked someone where the radios were, and then she and Benjamin went to that section of the store. She found a salesman (Victor, his White Front name tag said) and Benjamin showed him the ad in the magazine for the Sony transistor pocket radio. The salesman looked at the ad and then at Benjamin and said, "You're a very lucky boy, we only have two left. This thing is the hottest item we've had all year. Everyone wants it. They fly out of here like hotcakes." Benjamin thought about that sentence and wondered if Victor was related to his mother in some way. Victor went to a nearby display table and brought over two boxes.

"Here they are," Victor said. "They're both exactly the same, except for the color. Which one would you like, young man?"

Benjamin looked at the image on both boxes very carefully. One box showed the radio with a yellowish sort of top and a red-rimmed and gold tuning dial. The other box showed the radio with a green top and green-rimmed and gold tuning dial. He liked both of them and didn't quite know what to do about it.

"Well," Minnie asked. "Which one will it be?"

Benjamin scrunched up his face, looked back and forth and forth and back and then back and forth again. The salesman, Victor, with a bemused expression on his face, said, "The one with the red and yellow is the most popular."

That made up Benjamin's mind and he chose the yellow and red one. Besides, he thought that was the one that Susan would like best. Minnie paid for it, the salesman put the box in a White Front bag and off they went to the car.

Benjamin couldn't wait to get home and unbox his Sony transistor pocket radio, but by this time Minnie was hungry, so they stopped on the way home and had lunch at Van de Kamp's on Wilshire Blvd.

As soon as he got home, Benjamin opened the box and pulled out the radio. It was magnificent, just as he knew it would be. So shiny, so new, so small. The red and gold tuning dial was on the upper left, the on/off dial was on the edge of the right side, and at the bottom right of the gold grille was a little metal square that said Sony.

He inserted the special battery they'd bought, and then turned on the radio. It worked, and immediately he started rotating the tuner dial. The sound was excellent and the stations were coming in very clearly. He took the earphone out of its bag and plugged it in. Suddenly the radio was totally silent. Benjamin put the earphone in and suddenly music was playing in his ear. He had to turn the volume down a bit, because it was painfully loud. He sat cross-legged on his bed, flipping around the dial until he'd tuned in every station he possibly could.

Later that day, he ran over to Susan's to show it to her. She was going off to some dinner with her father, but she was suitably impressed by Benjamin's new transistor radio and gave it the Susan Seal of Approval.

Benjamin spent the rest of the day playing his new radio. That night, after dinner and television, he lay in bed and read the booklet that came with the radio from cover to cover. The official name of the radio was the Sony TR-63. He thought that a very good name for a transistor radio and assumed that the TR stood for transistor radio. He read that the radio had six transistors. He didn't know what a transistor was, but he thought six was a very good number to have in a transistor radio, certainly better than two or five. It said that it was imported from Japan and made by the Tokyo Tsushin Kogyo, Ltd. Company. That name was very exotic sounding and he was happy he'd chosen that brand instead of a plain old GE, Emerson or Philco.

Ernie came in the room and told Benjamin it was time for bed. Benjamin got under the covers and put the radio on the table by the bed. Ernie shut the light off and closed the door.

As soon as the door closed, Benjamin grabbed the radio, put the earphone in his ear and pulled the covers over his head. He turned it on and fiddled with the tuning dial until he found music. In his ear, Johnny Mathis gently crooned:

Chances are, 'cause I wear a silly grin
The moment you come into view

Benjamin was indeed wearing a silly grin and as the song continued he thought of Susan and thought of her kissing his cheek and he fell asleep with the radio on his chest and the earphone in his ear and Johnny Mathis singing

Bruce Kimmel

Chances are you'll believe the stars
That fill the skies
Are in my eyes

***

On July 4th, Susan called Benjamin and asked him if he'd like to go with her and her father to the Olympic Drive-In to see a movie and the 4th of July fireworks display. Benjamin thought that sounded like a splendid idea. He hated doing fireworks on Sherbourne Drive. Ernie would bring home sparklers and those little stupid snake things, and occasionally something that shot into the air that would invariably die a slow death before actually becoming fireworks. The whole Kritzer family would stand outside on the sidewalk along with all the other families that lined Sherbourne Drive, and they'd all hold sparklers, as if that were somehow festive and exciting. Also, Lee Adams, who lived in the house to the left of the Kritzers, had blown his pinkie off by lighting a firecracker and then holding it until it exploded. The Adams family was not known for its brainpower, and there was no telling what Lee Adams body part might be blown off this year and, frankly, Benjamin didn't want to be around to see it. So, he asked Ernie and Minnie if he could go and they said that since Jeffrey was going to a friend's house, they didn't see why Benjamin couldn't go to the drive-in to watch fireworks, as long as he wasn't home too late.

Benjamin walked over to Susan's, and she and her father were waiting for him by the garage in the alleyway. Hugo Pomeroy was a pleasant sort, blonde like his daughter, around five foot eight and thin as a rail. He pulled his pickup truck out of the garage and Benjamin and Susan got in and they drove north to Olympic, turned left and headed west. The sun was just setting and the sky was a beautiful purple. Benjamin and Susan chit-chatted about his new transistor radio (which, being a pocket transistor radio, was in his pocket), and Susan told Benjamin about her new favorite backwards words, olleh and eybdoog, which, to Benjamin, sounded like the cousins of Hansel and Gretel.

As they neared Sepulveda, they could see the sign of the Olympic Drive-In lit up in all its neon glory, with the rotating rainbow colors lighting each successive letter until they were all lit, then repeating the pattern. The Olympic was located on the northwest corner of Olympic and Bundy, and was Benjamin's favorite drive-in (he'd only been to two, but he liked this one better than the Gilmore because they had a play area in front of the movie screen). They pulled in, paid, and found a nice parking space about two lanes back from the screen. Hugo got out and set up two lawn chairs in the back of the truck for Benjamin and Susan to sit in. Hugo liked to sit by himself and stretch his legs across the seat of the truck.

Benjamin and Susan sat in their chairs, as the sun finally disappeared and darkness set in. Within minutes, the drive-in was filled to capacity. Hugo had hung the drive-in speaker on the back of the truck but near the driver's side window, so that they could all hear the sound. Susan had brought along a sack of goodies, including red licorice (from Marty's Bike and Candy Shop, naturally), a Three Musketeers bar, a pack of Blackjack gum and some Red Hots. Suddenly music blared forth from the tinny-sounding drive-in speaker and on the screen it said, "Welcome to the 4th of July fireworks show. Sit back and enjoy as we light up the sky. The main feature will begin right after the fireworks."

Benjamin opened the box of Red Hots and dumped about twenty of them in his mouth, then handed Susan the box and she did the same. Benjamin didn't really like Red Hots at all, but he did like the fact that they turned his tongue bright red. The fireworks started with a literal bang, with several loud bursts, and suddenly the sky was ablaze with color, spiraling, cascading all over the star-laden night sky. Whizzing and whistling noises accompanied each new explosion of color, and you could hear people clapping from different cars around the drive-in. Benjamin looked at Susan and stuck his bright red tongue out of his mouth. She looked back at him and stuck her bright red tongue out of her mouth, and they both laughed and poured more Red Hots into their mouths. The fireworks show lasted another ten minutes or so, and the final displays were the best of all—especially the red, white and blue one at the very end. By that time, the box of Red Hots was empty and had been tossed aside, and the two of them were now chewing Blackjack gum.

The main feature started (*Gunfight at the OK Corral*), and Benjamin and Susan sat in their lawn chairs and watched. Benjamin always thought it was strange to watch a movie at the drive-in where the sound didn't come from the screen. It was peculiar to not only hear the sound coming out the speaker attached to the truck, but to also hear it coming from other speakers around the drive-in, which created a weird kind of ambience. Susan didn't really care for westerns and she got restless, so instead of watching, they played the movie game (one person gave the initials of a movie and its star—FF starring AH—and the other person would try to guess it—*Funny Face* starring Audrey Hepburn), which they were both very good at.

Benjamin looked up at the stars and Susan followed his gaze as he did. He told her about his stars on the ceiling machine and how he'd lie in bed for hours staring at the constellations and galaxies. But seeing them like this, he saw that the machine couldn't hold a candle to the real thing—those beautiful twinkling bits of light in the pitch-black sky. They got off their chairs and lay on their backs in the bed of the truck, staring up at the stars. The night was balmy and the air was permeated with the smell of jasmine. Susan pointed at the sky and said, "Can you see that?"

Benjamin looked where she was pointing. "What?"

"Look. There are two stars there, all by themselves. See?"

Benjamin squinted and looked and finally saw what she was looking at. "Oh, yeah, there. I see them."

"They're ours. Those are the Benjamin and Susan stars and they don't belong to anyone but us."

She glanced at the window of the truck and saw that her father was looking straight ahead, engrossed in the movie. She leaned over and kissed Benjamin on the cheek like she'd done in front of Carolina Pines. It was just a little kiss, really, but to Benjamin it was like the fireworks show had started all over again and in his mind the sky was aglow with colors fizzing and swirling and zooming and showering down all around him. It was like that movie, *To Catch a Thief*, and Susan was Grace Kelly and Benjamin was Cary Grant and he wished Louie Wish were there with his Polaroid Land Camera so he could capture this moment forever.

CHAPTER SEVEN
The Hanger,
and Back To School

The rest of the summer flew by. Benjamin and Susan spent most days together, going everywhere and doing everything. They visited Farmer's Market (where they ate what-is-it-fish and Benjamin's favorite cole slaw), went to the May Company on Fairfax and Wilshire (where they rode the escalators up and down and down and up to each floor of the gigantic department store—in the furniture department there was a table with a chess set on it, and they sat there for an hour playing chess even though neither one of them knew the first thing about the game), went to Westwood and Beverly Hills, all thanks to Susan's expertise with bus schedules. By the end of the summer, she knew the unique Benjamin Kritzer's unique city of Los Angeles like the back of her well-held hand.

They saw many many movies at many many theaters. Not only the neighborhood ones, no, they went to the Picwood in West Los Angeles (eating two hamburgers each at Scot's next door); the Village in Westwood (one of Benjamin's favorites—where he'd originally seen *The High and the Mighty*, *The Tender Trap* and *The Robe*); to the El Rey, the Ritz and the Four Star, all on Wilshire Blvd.'s Miracle Mile; to the Wilshire and the Fine Arts (afterwards they ate at Dolores Drive-In across the street); to the Beverly in Beverly Hills (Benjamin liked that theater because of the Austin Healy clock next to the movie screen—the Beverly also had incredible stairs for Benjamin to roll down); and they went to the Stanley Warner Beverly Hills.

It was there that they saw *The Ten Commandments*, a movie that was even longer than *Giant*—in fact, it was close to four hours and longer than any movie that Benjamin had ever seen. It was an impressive movie, there was no doubt about that, but for some reason about two-and-a-half hours in, somewhere around the tenth time that Anne Baxter said, "Moses, Moses, Moses," Benjamin got the giggles, which caused Susan to get the giggles, and her getting the giggles caused Benjamin's giggles to double, and within minutes the two of them were laughing so hard it wasn't even funny (well, it *was* funny, that was the point). People were shushing them and giving them nasty looks and that only made things worse and made them laugh even harder. At one point, in the midst of her mad giggling, Susan leaned over to Benjamin and said, "This is a serious movie, we have to stop laughing." Of course, that only made them laugh harder. By the time that Moses was parting the Red Sea, Benjamin had literally fallen off his seat onto the floor and had tears streaming down his face, while Susan kept trying not to laugh and failing miserably. Somehow, they barely managed to get through the rest of the film without being tossed out of the theater.

***

Benjamin listened to his transistor radio constantly and every day would discover a new song he loved, which he would then have to go buy at Index Radio and Records. His collection of 45s was becoming very impressive and he had to buy an album to hold them all. Jeffrey had begun to study for his upcoming Bar Mitzvah, so Benjamin had to endure him reading his haftorah day in and day out and reading it quite badly in Benjamin's humble opinion.

***

One very hot Thursday, Benjamin got home around three o'clock. He and Susan had taken the bus to the beach and had spent the day sitting in the sand and watching the passing parade of kids, parents, teenagers, musclemen and old folks (sitting under beach umbrellas). They'd had corn dogs and lemonades and then taken the bus back home.

As Benjamin walked down the hall toward his bedroom, he heard his mother's voice coming from the kitchen, saying "Benjamin, come here." He did not like the tone in her voice; he did not like that tone one bit. He turned around and walked back to the kitchen. Minnie was sitting at the kitchen table as if she'd been sitting there all day just waiting for Benjamin to get home. He did not like the look on her face; he did not like that look one bit. She looked at him, her face a mass of agitation.

"Rosie Grubman called me today," she said, as if it had some important meaning. "She saw you today, you and your friend, walking down La Cienega."

"Yeah?" asked Benjamin, trying to understand where this was going. Of all his mother's friends, he liked Rosie Grubman the least.

"Do you know what she told me, Benjamin?"

"How would I know what she told you? She didn't call me, she called you."

"Don't you be a smart aleck!" Minnie's voice was rising to an uncomfortable level. She continued, "I'll tell you what she told me. She told me that you and that girl were holding hands, that's what she told me. What do you have to say for yourself?"

"We were holding hands. What's the big deal?"

Minnie stood up. "What's the big deal? I'll tell you what the big deal is, Benjamin. The big deal is that nine-year-old boys and girls don't hold hands, that's what the big deal is, Benjamin."

"Why?"

"Why? Because they don't. It's too young to hold hands. Why on earth would you be holding hands with that girl?"

"I like her? I like holding her hand? She's my friend."

Minnie's face started to crumble. "Friends don't hold hands like that. Rosie Grubman said you looked lovey-dovey. I mean, what is going on with this girl?"

Benjamin started to speak but Minnie kept right on going. "Next thing you know you'll be playing doctor."

"Playing doctor? What does that mean? How do you play doctor?"

"Never mind," Minnie said quickly.

"How do you play doctor?" Benjamin repeated.

"Never mind. I'm sorry I opened a can of worms."

"You opened a can of worms? They have canned worms?"

"Shut up! You know what I mean! I will not have you holding hands with this girl anymore. Do you understand me?"

"No, I don't understand you."

Minnie stormed to the hall closet. "You don't understand me? Maybe you need some help understanding me, maybe that's what you need!" Benjamin knew what was coming. She reached in the closet and took out a wooden hanger. He started to run toward his room but she was right there behind him. He tried closing the door on her, but she shoved it open and started hitting him with the hanger, over and over, on the arm, on the rear end, on the back. He tried to fend off the blows, but to little avail. She was practically screaming as she continued smacking him. "Now do you understand me? I DO NOT WANT YOU TO HOLD HANDS WITH THAT GIRL AGAIN DO I MAKE MYSELF PERFECTLY CLEAR?"

Benjamin started shaking and he too started screaming, "Stop it, stop it, stop it, stop it, stop it, stop it!"

"Don't you scream at me, don't you ever scream at me," she screamed, hitting him again. He finally just stood there, still shaking, but not crying, never crying. Minnie finally stopped and she started to cry. She was breathing heavily and her teeth were clattering around in her mouth. "What did I do to deserve a child like this?" she said to no one in particular. She threw the hanger across the room and stormed out, slamming the door behind her. Benjamin could hear her weeping loudly as she went to her room. He sat on the edge of the bed. His arms and back were still stinging from the repeated blows of the hanger. He sat there, wanting to cry, but refusing to give in to the tears that were hovering just behind his eyes. He picked up the transistor radio, put the earphone in his ear and turned it on. He twirled the dial slowly until he found a song he liked, Perry Como singing *Catch A Falling Star*. He sat there on the edge of the bed, motionless, listening.

Catch a falling star and put it in your pocket,
Never let it fade away…

He thought about Susan, about holding her hand and thought about what his mother would have done if she'd seen Susan kiss him on the cheek. That would have made her teeth fall right out of her mouth onto the floor.

Catch a falling star and put it in your pocket,
Save it for a rainy day…

Benjamin was still sitting on the edge of the bed an hour later when Ernie opened the door and came in. He walked over to the bed and said quietly, "Dinner's ready."

Benjamin didn't look up. "I'm not hungry."

"Would you like to eat in your room? It's meatloaf."

"Okay," said Benjamin.

"Your mother is sorry she lost her temper. You know how she gets. Benjamin, if you're going to hold hands make sure Rosie Grubman doesn't see you."

Ernie left the room, and a moment later brought Benjamin a big plate of meatloaf and mashed potatoes. He left the room and closed the door behind him. As Benjamin sat and ate the meatloaf (Minnie did make delicious meatloaf, he had to give her that, but just barely), he wondered why the phrase was "she lost her temper" instead of "she found her temper". Surely if you lost your temper you wouldn't have your temper. It was yet more folly on the part of the saying people, and another one for the Word Notebook. He started to chuckle as he took a big mouthful of meatloaf.

***

The final week before school started was hectic as usual, with new clothes to buy, new shoes to buy and new school supplies to buy. Benjamin got a brand new notebook (a nice blue one) and a goodly supply of lined notebook paper to put in it. He also got a nice plastic pen holder, some colorful dividers and an assortment of pens and pencils. He was not looking forward to school starting because he didn't know who his new teacher was going to be and because it meant he'd be spending less time with Susan.

They managed to catch one last weekday matinee at the Lido, *Invasion of the Saucermen* and *I Was a Teenage Werewolf*, a scare-fest which was scary only if you found people with big teeth and hair on their face scary, or Saucermen with big bulbous heads with big bulbous veins scary. In fact, the posters outside the theater were scarier than the movies, he thought.

Benjamin never told Susan about the incident and they held hands just like they always did, Rosie Grubman be damned. Rosie Grubman had, in fact, joined the Bad Men as somebody who should be totally avoided at all costs. Minnie seemed to have forgotten all about the incident and while the Kritzer household wasn't exactly harmonious, it was at least mercifully calm.

***

Benjamin picked Susan up on his way to school, as he always did, and they walked to Crescent Heights together. The first day of a new semester always made Benjamin uneasy. It was almost like he'd never gone to school before and everything was totally new and foreign to him. Susan (looking really cute in her new lavender dress and white sweater, white socks, black shoes and her blonde hair tied in a ponytail with a lavender ribbon) told Benjamin she'd see him at lunch and then went off to her new fifth grade class as Benjamin went off to his.

BENJAMIN KRITZER

It was worse than he imagined. Much worse. His new teacher, Miss Brady, was not nearly as nice as Mrs. Wallett. Not only was she not nearly as nice as Mrs. Wallett, she was the opposite: A pinched and severe looking woman, with gray hair done up tightly in a bun and the most sour expression Benjamin had ever seen. In fact, Benjamin thought, Miss Brady looked like she'd been sucking on a lemon for two years. It was no wonder she was *Miss* Brady; Benjamin couldn't imagine anyone wanting to come home and look at that expression every day. And, yet, he would be looking at that expression every day until next February, and if he had her again in A5 he'd be looking at it until next June.

Miss Brady was no-nonsense and quite stern even while calling roll. She was so stern, in fact, that when Monty Presser made one of his jokes when his name was called, she turned to him with an icy stare and said, "Not in my classroom, young man—we do not joke in my classroom. One more joke out of you and you will be joking in Mrs. Peck's office." She even gave them homework to do. Benjamin couldn't remember ever having homework on the first day of a new semester. No, it was quite clear that the fifth grade was not going to be a barrel of laughs.

***

School days were long and endless, and by the third week Benjamin could barely listen to Miss Brady's nasal droning voice go on and on about things he couldn't have cared less about. He daydreamed constantly and she caught him at it constantly. He'd be staring out the schoolroom window having the nicest thoughts (mostly about Susan), when suddenly he'd hear that awful voice saying, "Benjamin Kritzer, would you like to join the rest of us or would you like to daydream in Mrs. Peck's office?" or "Benjamin Kritzer, I'm sure we'd all like to be staring out the window instead of doing our schoolwork—I asked you a question and I haven't heard the answer," and of course Benjamin had no clue as to what the question had been or what the answer should be.

But then there was recess or lunch or after school and those brief times were always spent with Susan. Other kids started to make fun of them. "Ooh, look at the two lovebirds" they'd say, or "Benjamin and Susan sitting in a tree, k-i-s-s-i-n-g." Of course Benjamin and Susan weren't sitting in a tree and they were hardly k-i-s-s-i-n-g (not that he would have minded, no, that would have been fine by him), so what the point of that silly rhyme was was beyond him.

Of course, they had weekends, and they still went to movies and went to Leo's (he'd always greet them with "There's my two favorite customers!") and took buses and went places like the La Brea Tar Pits (Benjamin presumed there not only had to be dinosaur bones in the tar pits but that there had to be rat bones in the tar pits, too, because "rat" was "tar" spelled backwards), the Pan Pacific auditorium (Elvis was going to play there on October 23rd), and Westlake Park (Susan made them sack lunches and they sat on the grass and ate while they watched people boating on the lake); but then the weekend would be over and the drudgery of five school days (and attendant homework) would start all over again. The kids continued to tease Benjamin and Susan and they continued not to care.

After school one Wednesday afternoon, Benjamin was sitting in the den watching television (he should have been doing homework) when the phone rang. He heard Lulu answer it (Minnie was out playing cards with "the girls"), "Kritzer residence" and then a moment later she bellowed, "Benjamin, it's your girlfriend," and then howled with laughter. Benjamin went to the kitchen and took the phone from Lulu, who said, "My, my, my" and left to go finish the ironing. Susan asked if he could meet her at Robertson Playground at four-thirty. He asked if anything was wrong, and she said no, just that she had something she wanted to do.

At four-thirty sharp (Benjamin, like Susan, was always very punctual), Benjamin entered Robertson Playground. It was fairly large as playgrounds went, and it had basketball courts, some benches, tetherball, and a building with an indoor court and a little stage. There were also swings and sandboxes and a handful of trees. He looked around and saw Susan leaning up against a small tree and he went over to her. The park was empty except for some teenagers shooting baskets way on the other end. She said, "Hi. Help me up, I want to sit on that branch." There was a sturdy long branch jutting out not too high from the ground. She stood on the bench next to the tree, and Benjamin helped her climb up to the branch.

"Now you come up," she said. He stood on the bench and climbed up and squeezed next to her. It wasn't too comfortable but certain things were worth discomfort, one of them being sitting next to Susan.

"What's going on?" he asked. She smiled at him and her eyes twinkled.

"Benjamin and Susan sitting in a tree, k-i-s-s-i-n-g." She leaned over and gave him a kiss on the cheek. Then, quite out of the blue, she took his head and turned it toward her and kissed him right on the mouth, just like that, no warning at all. He almost fell right out of the tree and she had to hold on to him. "There," she said. "Now when they tease us they'll be telling the truth."

They sat there for another ten minutes, precariously perched on the branch of the tree, not a care in the world, letting the cool afternoon breeze wash over them.

Afterwards, he walked her home.

CHAPTER EIGHT
Fall Back

October brought rainstorms, and they lasted all throughout the month. There was lightning and thunder and strangest of all, hail, huge nuggets of hail. Benjamin didn't see Susan as much, because recesses were canceled and lunch was eaten inside the classroom. He still walked her to and from school, though, and still saw her on weekends. Daylight Savings Time ended and Minnie methodically turned all the clocks back one hour ("Spring Forward, Fall Back," she said) and it now got dark by five.

On Halloween, Benjamin and Susan went trick or treating together. She went as an old crone, complete with a wart on her cheek (a big piece of gum wadded up) and a pointy nose and pointy hat, and Benjamin went as a ghoul, with a green face and Five Day Deodorant Pads over his eyes (he could see out the tiny hole in the middle of them). They got all kinds of goodies—Jujubes, Snickers, Milky Ways, Baby Ruths, marshmallows, Butter-Nuts, Cherry-A-Lets, and lots more. They ate quite a bit of their bounty that very night and both of them were quite nauseous, not to mention quite hyper.

***

A week later the rains had stopped and Los Angeles was its usual sunny self. School was a continual ordeal, and Miss Brady seemed to get worse as the weeks went by. The three o'clock bell couldn't come fast enough for Benjamin.

***

On the second Friday in November Benjamin arrived at Susan's house to pick her up in the morning. She wasn't waiting outside like usual, so he went up the stairs and knocked on the door. There was no answer, so he knocked again, louder. Still no answer. He got a nervous feeling in the pit of his stomach, because something had to be wrong. Well, maybe she'd woken up with a tummy ache or a headache or some other kind of ache, and maybe her father had taken her to the doctor, although she hadn't looked or acted sick the day before. Or maybe she had a dentist appointment or something like that, although he was pretty sure she would have mentioned it. He knocked one more time, but it was obvious that no one was home. He walked to school, quite concerned and worried.

She wasn't there at recess. At lunch, Benjamin went to their usual meeting place, hoping she'd be there, but she was nowhere to be found. She must have been sick, because she still wasn't there at three o'clock when school ended.

By this time, he was very concerned, and he ran the few blocks to her house, went down the alley, walked up the back steps and knocked on the door. After a moment, the door opened and there stood Susan, tears streaming down her face. Benjamin had never seen anything but Susan's sunny disposition and her amazing smile, so seeing her like this was a shock.

"What's wrong? I got worried. Are you sick?"

She looked at Benjamin for a long time. "We're moving again," she finally said, the tears streaming down her pink cheeks.

Benjamin felt like he had when his brother had punched him really hard in the stomach—he couldn't breathe, felt as if he'd never be able to breathe again.

"Why?"

"My father got transferred again. He just found out and they want him there on Monday."

"Monday? Next Monday? There where?"

"Canada. Montreal, Canada. Next Monday. We're leaving tomorrow. I'm nine years old and I've already lived in twelve different places. Benjamin, I don't want to leave." And with that, the tears multiplied and began to resemble running tap water.

Benjamin stood there, unable to speak. He didn't really know where Canada was; in fact the only Canada he knew was Canada Dry Ginger Ale. But it sounded far away, sounded like an eternity away, a lifetime away, an "I'll never see you again" away. From inside, Susan's father called out, "Susan, say whatever you've got to say, we've got a lot of packing to do."

Susan suddenly threw herself into Benjamin's arms and hugged him tightly. "Oh, Benjamin," she said, her voice muffled because her mouth was pressed against his sweater.

"You can't go," said Benjamin. "If you go to Canada I'll never see you again."

"What can I do? I'm nine, parents don't listen to nine-year-old children."

"Susan…"

That's all Benjamin could muster, the words simply wouldn't come out. He knew there were words that needed to come out but he couldn't make them. Instead he held on to Susan tightly. From inside, Susan's father called again, this time impatiently.

As hard as it was, Susan pulled herself away. "I've got to go, Benjamin. I'll send you my address. At least we can write each other." She handed him an envelope. "Here."

Benjamin looked at the envelope and then at her, looked at this beautiful nine-year-old person with whom he'd become inseparable, looked at this person he would most likely never see again and he did something which surprised even him—he grabbed Susan and kissed her full on the mouth, kissed her for all he was worth, kissed her and tasted the sweetness of her mouth mixed with the saltiness of her tears.

"Susan," her father bellowed. "Don't make me say your name again."

"Don't forget about me, Benjamin."

"Forget about you? How could I ever forget about you?"

Her tears would not stop. "I've got to go in." She turned toward the door, then turned back to him. "I love you, Benjamin Kritzer."

He wasn't sure anyone had ever said those words to him. Certainly he couldn't remember his parents ever saying them. He stood there, his heart in his throat and finally said, "I love you."

And with that she was gone, the door closing behind her sounding much too final.

Benjamin went down the steps slowly and then walked down the alleyway and onto Airdrome and toward his house. He wanted to cry, but crying was something he'd conditioned himself not to do. Benjamin Kritzer simply didn't cry, whether he was being hit with a hanger or yelled at or punished. And yet, there he was, suddenly crying, tears welling up and spilling out of his eyes—because he would never again walk Susan Pomeroy home, never again see her beautiful face or see her blonde hair blowing in the breeze, never again share red licorice from Marty's Bike and Candy Shop, never again hear her voice or her mad giggle, which always made him smile. Oh, yes, he cried and when he got home he went directly to his room, shut the door, and cried some more. No more holding hands, no more discovering places together, no more sitting in the movies with her scratching his arm, no more spelling backwards or talking on the phone or meeting at recess and lunch.

He had no appetite and at dinner just picked at the food on his plate. Minnie thought he had a fever and gave him some Aspergum and told him to lie down. Mercifully, Jeffrey was at a friend's house, so Benjamin had the room to himself.

At bedtime, he finally took out the envelope Susan had given him. "For Benjamin" was written on the front of it in her nice handwriting. He opened it and took out the folded piece of lined notebook paper, which he unfolded carefully. Some of the ink had smeared a tiny bit, as if her tears had fallen on the paper as she wrote. He switched on the record player, put *Young Love* on and read her letter.

Dear Benjamin:

I don't know how to write what I'm feeling. I'm supposed to be packing so it can't be a long letter. The first day you came up to me and said hi Benjamin Kritzer 4th grade, Mrs. Wallett's class, I knew I liked you. You made me laugh and you made me feel special. I don't know how I'll stand not seeing you, not going places with you. I will think of you all the time and I will never never forget you. I hope you will think of me, too, and never never forget me. I have been crying all day and I can't stop. I have to go now, but I wanted you to know that I went to the gas station with my father to fill his truck up and I saw the best backwards word ever – saglibom. Please add it to our book, Nimajneb. I will write you and send you my address and then we can send letters to each other. I want to say so many things to you but I have to stop writing now. I'm scratching your arm now, can you feel it?

    Love forever,
    Susan (Nasus)

Benjamin pressed the letter to his face as if that would make it seem like she was close to him. *Young Love* finished playing and he reached back and shut the machine off. He read the letter three more times then carefully folded it back up and put it in the envelope, which he then placed in the pocket of their Word Notebook. He shut the light off and got into bed. He thought about the song he used to sing to cheer himself up.

When the red red robin
Comes bob bob bobbin' along, along
There'll be no more sobbin' when he starts throbbin'
His old sweet song…

He suspected it was going to be a very long time before the red red robin would ever be bob bob bobbin' again.

***

Benjamin was blue. That was the color his mother had ascribed to him—he was also, according to her, down in the dumps. He wondered who had decided that blue should be the color for being down in the dumps, instead of green or purple or yellow, but, of course, his mother had no answer, only that blue was down in the dumps, green was envy, red was anger and yellow was cowardly. Purple, apparently, was just a color.

Everywhere he went, whether to school, to Leo's Delicatessen, to the movies, to the Orange Julius stand—nothing felt right to him without Susan being there. He felt like he'd lost half of himself. Leo was very understanding, which is more than Benjamin could say for his parents, who merely told him to forget about her. That was not going to be happening, though. There would be no forgetting about Susan Pomeroy.

Every time Benjamin had to walk by Susan's duplex, more often than not he'd end up walking down the familiar alley to the familiar back stairs and there he'd sit, back against the garage that faced the duplex, and stare at the door where he'd had his final glimpse of Susan. Stare, as if any moment Susan would come bounding out of the door and off they'd go to the movies, or to have an Orange Julius or to simply hold hands. But, of course, she never bounded out of the door because another family lived there now.

He checked the mailbox every day but nothing ever arrived. For some time he believed that maybe the Bad Men had taken the letter or that it had somehow gotten stuck in the upper portion of the mailbox as some letters did. He began having dreams that he would find her letter stuck in the upper portion of the mailbox and in his dreams they would meet again and be together forever.

***

The Kritzers went to Uncle Lenny and Aunt Bertha's for Thanksgiving, but Benjamin didn't feel like giving thanks because he felt miserable. Everyone had a fine time, and his cousins Arthur and Marty tried to cheer him up by playing pink belly with him (a rather inane game which consisted of slapping someone's stomach until it was pink). He only smiled once the whole evening, and that was when someone at the table said, "May I have a yam?" and Benjamin immediately thought, of course you may have a yam because may *is* yam spelled backwards. He knew Susan would have loved that.

CHAPTER NINE
The Winter of His Discontent

Benjamin was slowly being driven insane. Jeffrey was studying for his Bar Mitzvah and had learned the entire haftorah, which he sang day in and day out, over and over again. It was painful, rather like Moe poking Curley in the eyes with his fingers or ripping out some of Larry's hair, and Benjamin avoided Jeffrey whenever possible.

Benjamin had his tenth birthday and, although he got some nice presents, all he could think about was how much fun it would have been to celebrate it with Susan. They most certainly would have gone to the movies and she most certainly would have bought him the best present and she most certainly would have scratched his arm and she might have even most certainly kissed him. It was an important birthday—Benjamin had made it to ten and now had two digits in his age, which he felt was quite an accomplishment. He was still unique, which he also felt was quite an accomplishment.

That night he sat in the backyard, found the Benjamin and Susan stars and knew that she was somehow there with him and it made him feel that his tenth year was going to be okay. He wondered if she could also see the two stars from wherever she was in far off Montreal, Canada.

***

Jeffrey's Bar Mitzvah went off without a hitch, and there was a big party at the Sportsmen's Lodge in the Valley. Everyone danced (except Benjamin), everyone kvelled (except Benjamin), and everyone sang *Hava Nagila* (except Benjamin). Jeffrey had a throng of thirteen-year-old girls there and he was the life of the party with all of them. When the candle-lighting part took place, Jeffrey handed the taper first to Minnie, who lit her candle, and then to Ernie, who lit his. Benjamin walked forward to take the taper and Jeffrey thrust it at him almost burning Benjamin's eyeball with it. A photographer happened to capture that moment for all time and there was now living proof that his brother was a foorp and trying to kill him. It was one of Benjamin's favorite pictures.

***

Even though Bing Crosby was dreaming of a *White Christmas*, Benjamin was most decidedly having a Blue Christmas. He missed Susan and there was no consoling him. He looked in the mailbox every day and every day there was nothing for him. He tried calling information in Montreal, Canada, to see if he could get an address or phone number for her, but they had no listing.

On Christmas, he opened his presents, tried to feign enthusiasm but unfortunately wasn't very convincing. Christmas afternoon they all trundled down to Ocean Park to give Grandma and Grandpa Gelfinbaum their presents. Grandma Gelfinbaum's idea of a present for Benjamin and Jeffrey was giving them gold-wrapped chocolate gelt shaped like fifty-cent pieces. Ocean Park Pier was entirely boarded up, and peering through the space in the boards across from the St. Regis, Benjamin could see the skeleton of what was being touted as Neptune's Kingdom, the entrance to Pacific Ocean Park.

***

Whenever Benjamin felt really blue, he took out Susan's letter and read it again and again. It made him sad, but it also made him happy and as he'd read it he could almost see her and hear her mad giggle; it was almost as if she were right there next to him.

***

1958 arrived and with it no letter from Susan.

Christmas vacation was over and Benjamin was back in school, enduring Miss Brady once again. Christmas hadn't done a thing to make her a person of good cheer. If Christmas was white, and Benjamin was blue, he decided a good color for Miss Brady would be burnt sienna (he got that name from a crayon). Burnt sienna just suited Miss Brady to a "t". Of course, no one was teasing Benjamin about sitting in a tree and k-i-s-s-i-n-g, although he wished they were.

He couldn't shake the blue feeling, nor did he want to shake the blue feeling, because if he shook the blue feeling then it would somehow lessen how much he pined for Susan. He simply was not the old Benjamin, he was Gloomy Gus according to Minnie and, frankly, she was becoming very tired of it.

She finally confronted him one day when he came home from school.

"When are you going to stop walking around the house like someone died?" she asked impatiently.

Benjamin had no answer, so he started to go to his room.

"Stop right there, I'm talking to you. Stop crying over spilt milk, Benjamin."

Benjamin turned around slowly and looked at his mother. "What? What?"

"You heard me. She's gone, Benjamin, and that's all there is to it. So stop crying over spilt milk."

It was all too much for Benjamin and he began to yell. "I'm not crying over spilt milk! I *hate* milk! I would *laugh* over spilt milk! What a stupid saying! Who would cry over spilt milk anyway?"

"Exactly," said Minnie. "And stop yelling!"

Benjamin quickly changed the subject. "Was there any mail?"

"Yes, there was mail. Not for you." She'd totally lost her patience. "You know, Benjamin, just because she sent one letter doesn't mean…" She stopped abruptly.

Benjamin froze. "What did you say?"

Minnie looked down. "Nothing."

"You said she sent one letter. What do you mean she sent one letter? She sent a letter?"

Minnie turned away.

"Did I get a letter?" Benjamin asked again, his voice sounding like it didn't belong to a ten-year-old.

Minnie wheeled around. "Yes, you got a letter, okay? I tore it up."

Benjamin stood there, stunned. "You what?"

"I tore it up."

Benjamin began to tremble. "You tore it up? My letter? You tore up my letter?" His voice was up an entire octave, and now he was screaming as he had never screamed before. "When? When did it come?"

"At the end of November. It was for your own good, Benjamin. I thought the best thing you could do was to just forget about her."

"You thought the best thing I could do was just forget about her so you tore up my letter? I hate you! I hate you, I hate you!"

"Don't you dare talk to me that way! Don't you dare! I'm your mother, Benjamin, I think I know what's best for you!"

Benjamin's head felt like it was going to explode. "You're not my mother, you're a Martian! If you're my mother, show me my baby pictures! Why aren't there any baby pictures of me?"

Minnie just stood there, dumbfounded. Benjamin couldn't stop himself. "What's the matter, cat got your tongue?"

"That's enough! I've had enough of you!"

"You've had enough of *me*! I've had enough of *you*! How could you tear up my letter?"

"I'm warning you to shut up! Do not speak to me this way! She's gone and that's all there is to it! Forget about her!"

Benjamin reached deep inside and pulled out the worst thing he could think of. "Go to hell! I'm never forgetting about her!"

Minnie turned apple-red. "Go to hell? You will not speak to me like that!" She went to the hall closet and got out the wooden hanger. "You will apologize right now!"

"*You* apologize! You're the one who tore up my letter!"

She hit him across the arm with the hanger, the thwack echoing around the room. She went to hit him again, but he grabbed the hanger away from her. She was totally unprepared for that and just stood there in mid-swing, looking like some character in a cartoon. By this point he was so angry that he'd lost any semblance of sanity and he suddenly hit her across her arm with the hanger and it broke in two, one half of the hanger remaining in his hand, the other half clattering to the floor. The two of them stood there in shock, neither of them believing what had just happened.

Benjamin said quietly, "You will never hit me again, ever."

Minnie stood there for a full minute, and then she began to scream and pull at her hair. "What did I do to deserve this?" She started hitting herself on the arm and she wept and screamed, "What kind of child did

I raise?" She ran from the room, crying and screaming and continued pummeling her own arms. Benjamin heard her dialing the phone and then heard her muffled voice saying, "Your son hit me with a hanger! You come home right now!"

Benjamin went to his room and shut the door. There was already a big red welt on his arm, which he looked at curiously. He sat on his bed, heart pounding. And then he smiled. Smiled because he knew that Susan had written to him after all. Smiled because he knew with a certainty that she was in Montreal, Canada, and she was thinking about him and remembering him and missing him, and he hoped and prayed that she knew he was thinking about her and remembering her and missing her.

Of course there was a big scene when Ernie got home, with much breast-beating and yelling and crying (not Benjamin) and of course Benjamin was punished for his terrible behavior. It was worth it, though, because he knew down deep that Minnie would never hit him again.

He got in bed and turned on the stars. He turned on the transistor radio and put the earphone in his ear. He rotated the dial aimlessly, looking for a station that was playing something he liked. He couldn't stop thinking about the letter she'd written that he would never see. He wondered what it had said, wondered how she was doing in Montreal, Canada, and wondered if she'd ever write again.

Benjamin looked at the stars on the ceiling, the same stars he'd seen hundreds of times. And there, off to the right, were two single stars that he hadn't ever noticed before. They were snuggled next to each other with no other stars around them and there was no doubt in his mind that they were the Benjamin and Susan stars, just like the ones they'd found in the real sky.

He kept turning the dial until he finally heard the soothing and romantic voice of Johnny Mathis, who was singing his new hit song. Benjamin fell in love with it immediately.

You ask how much I need you,
Must I explain?
I need you oh my darling
Like roses need rain
You ask how long I'll love you
I'll tell you true
Until the Twelfth of Never
I'll still be loving you.

For the first time in quite a while Benjamin felt happy. He felt happy because he knew that no matter what happened, no matter what the future might bring, that he would never ever forget Susan Pomeroy. He would remember her until the Twelfth of Never.

EPILOGUE
Spring Forward

When Benjamin came out of the Picfair Theater the sun was already setting. He walked west on Pico, breathing the sweet-smelling air and looking at a sky ablaze with zillions of sunset colors. He looked around to see if the Bad Men were following him, but there was no one there.

He passed the Mobilgas Station at Pico and La Cienega, and as he did he looked up at the big sign that towered above him. Benjamin smiled wistfully because Mobilgas was, of course, the last backwards word Susan had written and was the final entry in their Word Notebook: saglibom.

As he headed towards Leo's Delicatessen to have a pickle and a soda pop, he thought about the last year—the year of Susan Pomeroy, the year that Ocean Park Pier had closed, the year he'd taken the hanger from his mother; and it suddenly occurred to him that his life was like one of those Saturday matinee movie serials he so loved—every week a new chapter with new adventures and thrills and Bad Men and romance and a cliffhanger ending. Yes, it seemed that life was just like the title card that came up at the end of every chapter:

To be continued...

ACKNOWLEDGMENTS

First and foremost, I'd like to thank Margaret Willock Jones for her unending support, kindness and enthusiasm, which made finishing this book a possibility; Cary Mansfield, for making sure the songs and the dates matched up; David Levy; Lisa Okikawa; the lovely and wonderful Susan Gordon; Grant Geissman for all his help; Dee Dee Feinberg, Adryan Russ, Laura and Sandra Miller, for their excellent comments and suggestions. And a huge thanks to Bruce Bunner and Sandy Powell of 1st Books for their unwavering support and good nature in dealing with a crazed first-time author.

Ingrid Tulean is, of course, the Swedish actress Ingrid Thulin, who had her name phonetically spelled Tulean, for both the film and posters of *Foreign Intrigue*.

And finally, a special acknowledgment to the house on Sherbourne Drive—I wonder if the Bad Men are still there rifling through the china cabinet. What is it, fish?

Bruce Kimmel

ABOUT THE AUTHOR

Bruce Kimmel has had a long and varied career. He wrote, directed and starred in the cult movie hit, *The First Nudie Musical*. He performed those same duties on his second film *The Creature Wasn't Nice* (a.k.a. *Naked Space*), with Leslie Nielsen, Cindy Williams and Patrick Macnee. He also co-created the story for the hit film, *The Faculty*, directed by Robert Rodriguez. As an actor, Mr. Kimmel has guest-starred on most of the long-running television shows of the Seventies, including *Happy Days*, *Laverne and Shirley*, *The Partridge Family*, *The Donny and Marie Show* and many others.

Since 1993, Mr. Kimmel has been the leading producer of theater music on CD, having produced more than one hundred and twenty-five albums. He was nominated for a Grammy for producing the revival cast album of *Hello, Dolly!* and his album with jazz pianist Fred Hersch, *I Never Told You*, was also nominated for a Grammy. He created the critically acclaimed *Lost In Boston* and *Unsung Musicals* series, has produced solo albums for Petula Clark, Helen Reddy, Liz Callaway, Laurie Beechman, Paige O'Hara, Christiane Noll, Judy Kaye, Judy Kuhn, Brent Barrett, Jason Graae, Randy Graff, Emily Skinner and Alice Ripley, and has worked with such legends as Lauren Bacall, Elaine Stritch and Dorothy Loudon. He has also produced many off-Broadway and Broadway cast albums, including the hit revival of *The King and I*, starring Lou Diamond Philips and Donna Murphy, *The Best Little Whorehouse In Texas* starring Ann-Margret and *Bells Are Ringing* starring Faith Prince.

Benjamin Kritzer is Mr. Kimmel's first novel.

Printed in the United States
766300001B